Tea Party

—— and the ——

Second Civil War

What happened to America?

RICHARD D. ONDO

iUniverse, Inc.
New York   Bloomington

Tea Party and the Second Civil War
What happened to America?

iUniverse books may be ordered through booksellers or by contacting:

iUniverse
1663 Liberty Drive
Bloomington, IN 47403
www.iuniverse.com
1-800-Authors (1-800-288-4677)

Because of the dynamic nature of the Internet, any Web addresses or links contained in this book may have changed since publication and may no longer be valid. The views expressed in this work are solely those of the author and do not necessarily reflect the views of the publisher, and the publisher hereby disclaims any responsibility for them.

ISBN: 978-1-4502-4964-5 (pbk)
ISBN: 978-1-4502-4966-9 (cloth)
ISBN: 978-1-4502-4965-2 (ebk)

Printed in the United States of America

iUniverse rev. date: 8/16/2010

Forward

Tea Party and the Second Civil War

His eloquent speeches made people drop to their knees in awe. Some reached out to touch him. Even his defeated campaign opponents applauded his arrival. Fan and followers were clapping for his well crafted campaign and rise to power. A virtual unknown candidate comes charging to the front of the pack, overcoming the stalwarts. It was a remarkable feat. An Illinois Senator with no measureable record becomes the president.

Unlike the first Republican President, Abraham Lincoln, the first black president was from the opposite party. Unlike President Lincoln, who brought the country together, the new top gun was a divider.

Two parties, Republican and Democrats, squandered the country's wealth by way of war and stimulus bills. The country's citizens had seen enough. A new force was forming, the Tea Party was born. American history was ready to be penned.

An economic look back at recessions and depressions would uncover the reason for new party leadership.

The State of Illinois had one mighty big city within its borders. Chicago grew when the railroad reached the city. The year was 1848, population, thirty thousand. Chicago had a dubious reputation in politics. Some say unsavory methods were used to acquire power in the city. After World War One the roaring twenties produced notorious Chicago outlaws.

A stock market crash in 1929 caused presidents to enable austerity programs to heal high unemployment. Those programs only lengthened the dismal dreg and didn't do much to restore employment. World War Two provided employment at a huge cost to humanity. The twenty-first century was trying to duplicate the past.

Change was coming to repeat history lessons. New iconoclasts had a vision for America and Europe. Many voters fell into the trap and gave permission to install narcissistic rulers to oversee America's wealth. The result was one party rule which acted like a dead weight on the nation's economy. A republic without political balance was unusual for a capitalistic society.

Born in the middle 1900's were two economic dynamos to work on enabling history to repeat. A Hungarian and an Italian communicated often enough to form a loose alliance.

After some incubating in California and Oregon as family director of hotel and casino operations, a power struggle forced Julius Cambello to flee the West Coast. Dispirited, the executive found a new opportunity in banking. Mid America was a proving ground as he gained power in Chicago.

He gathered steam in the banking industry as a hatchet man for cutting down failed businesses. He became a notorious cutthroat, a white collar executive, and political godfather. It didn't take long before he took control of the Chicago mob although he appeared to be Prince Charming. As a respected businessman he wormed his way into the financial operations of political action groups. His own political aspirations didn't work out, but he learned how to eliminate competition.

Fair play wasn't in his rule book. Rising like Al Capone, he gained the reigns as the new mob chief. Pushing his way into illegal activity, he used lieutenants to do the dirty work.

He culled government unions to use his bank and banking expertise. Campaign funds found safe haven in his bank. The result, he was responsible for creating political paper tigers. Using these pawns to enhance his wealth, stoke union deposits, and buy other banks. A South Chicago banking empire was building.

Gambling was a favorite recreation. To the godfather a fine cigar and a blackjack wager were the joys of life. Legal gambling or not it was one industry that he worshiped. Banking was secondary and according to his legacy, he was destined to be the leader in the gambling world.

One key to some of his success was finding a like-minded person. That was done early when a European partner was found. Several years of long exchanges with George Budapest, who also had a magic wand for making good investments, cemented cooperation. While vacationing in Europe, Cambello cut business deals with the billionaire Hungarian. Mr. Budapest's fortune and wizardry were spooned out of the European stock market. He mastered deals that extracted billions from the London Stock Exchange.

Chapter 1

POLITICAL STRATEGY

They worked on a 'New Deal' as if harnessing the inspiration of President Franklin Delano Roosevelt.

Cambello tells George, "I know the political landscape. I found the proverbial political Trojan horse. Into the White House, he sits, George."

George Budapest says, "You're not a Greek."

Cambello replies, "You helped me pave the way for these political knights. The top man, he uses czars as shields. They're part of his problem but gold will spike and that's the key for us."

George says, "You used a good deal of Magyar money. This better pay off.

Cambello counters, "Your money bought us the political tools. If we're right, we'll end up driving the price of gold through the roof."

The strategy was a good one. America and Europe both had financial problems brought about by their own greed. After the vacation George calls to announce his appreciation for the way thing are going in America.

George says, "I think you're right."

Cambello says, "Oh, George, I'm right."

George says, "I'll use this euphemism. It does look like you finally got something to grow. You're finally shaking America's money tree. The political fruits and nuts are spending money on hopeless programs just like the Russians."

Cambello says, "George, stimulus programs, it's Roosevelt all over again. I prayed this would happen."

The two men were financial gurus and shared a behind the scene strategy to elect political candidates that nourished their voluminous fortunes. Some politicians were elected in Europe and the largest share in the US. They built a political machine that bilked billions and billions of taxpayer money from the United States and Europe.

Julius Cambello was a likeable Chicago banker. It was a perfect disguise. His well developed empire was nurtured by taking control of the Chicago underworld. It took time, but it wasn't a foot race.

Racketeering, extortion, and loan sharking were early methods to take command of a few banks. In a little over ten years he commandeered and organized the Chicago syndicate. Ruthless in his manner he cleared a path to a multitude of legal and illegal businesses.

Julius and George worked on a plan to take control of the world's financial market. Julius told his billionaire friend a secret about the rising political star.

Mr. Cambello says, "He's a rubber neck, George, not a leather neck. He couldn't command a troop of cub scouts. However, the people around him are showing him the way. He's surrounded himself with czars. It'll be off their mistakes that we solve the world's problems."

Each man lifted their wine glasses and toasted each other. They leaned on each other for their ingenuity. A dynasty was in the making. Of the two men one claimed fame from ghastly underworld deals. The Hungarian, he masterfully played the stock market at the right time. They wanted more.

The president was merely skipping into the White House, because no serious contender was at the forefront. Major conflict was over. Only a mop up drill remained in Iraq and the Afghanistan Taliban was no match for US and UN forces.

The president's public credentials were guarded secrets, but that didn't seem to matter. People liked what they saw, but he was a pawn of the two billionaires. They rarely linked to each other because of the continental divide. Even their political lines didn't run straight. Chicago politics and European politics had some minor similarities. Julius and George's social joints were lubricated by using other people's money. This was the common bond.

They both spoke in glowing terms of helping America and Europe return to prosperity. Their political method might well be called a legalized national pick-pocket operation. The political scam of the century - was having a hand in the pocket of American and European businesses.

The president was ready to spread the wealth of America by piping the right music to the American public and the Europeans.

The United States president had a personal goal, spreading the wealth of America. He was a political marvel. The dramatic campaign speeches stated his goal of spreading the wealth along with unifying the nation. His coronation drove a wedge into the heart and soul of American society.

The European man, he dropped out of sight. His job was done. The other man had far more greatness on his mind. He was going after a bigger prize.

The president didn't get close to the bank owner. Julius was like a distant star. Like Pluto or a stepfather far removed from the son, he never got close to his son. Since they didn't know each other, no one would ever be hurt by his metaphoric odorless conniving. Only the wind of change would carry the monoxide to poison American society.

The uttered words were habit forming and hooked the citizens like a cocaine addiction. The president used his fans euphoria and adulation cleverly. He sold the fruit of hope and change.

The speech writers were effective. They conditioned the thoughts. The president used the teleprompters well. Staff writers convinced both Democrats and Republicans they could trust and abide by his level headedness.

The man behind the scene was the banker. He was the brain trust. By using the power of money Cambello influenced the country's decision makers.

The men and a president failed to realize that the enemies of America were watching like hawks on a wire. They included Asian leaders, Middle East dictators, terrorists, and homegrown subversives. An inside plot was being formulated. A plot to take over the government by coup was the goal. It was only just starting. Many ingredients had to fall in place. The adversaries had their own problems. So many factions despised America's freedom. They couldn't even trust each other.

China had the money. The terrorists desired a spiritual gateway to heaven. The dictators lacked the fire power.

The president was carrying a torch lit in Chicago. The country had to be cut down to size and the Constitution burned. The country had to be divided by internal infighting. This would start the downfall. The political divide would color states red and blue. It would be similar to the first civil war. In time it would be the start of the second civil war. The great divider would topple the United States of America.

Once divided, the terrorists would cause the first diversion using border raids. Public fear would lead to mini-armies and militias to form their own protection. Martial law would be called out. The leader, he would assume power. A new form of government would be ruling America.

The one factor not considered was the evolution of the Tea Party.

Chapter 2

RADICALS LEADERS

Fanatical leaders in third world countries were buying arms and trying to manufacture a dirty bomb. Iran was busy making the nuclear weapon which was a major goal to extort a favorable outcome in negotiations. Additionally, sending their agents to America to imbed at the universities would inflame anarchy. They could use the terrorists to inflict discourse and create confusion at the colleges. These were necessary steps to overthrow the republic and assume power.

It was their ultimate goal. The entire movement would overwhelm homeland security. Then the next faze would happen. Bombings in the cities would create panic. America would fall step by step. Each state would have to set up a self government.

The second civil war was forming. It was all being done right in front of congress.

Members of congress couldn't see the extent of the plan. Blinded by the benefits bestowed on elected officials, they were to busy expanding their authority by passing expensive social bills and living the good life. Their perch was high above the subjects.

The rulers faced a dilemma every so often. Trying to stay in office was becoming the biggest priority rather than shepherding the country.

America was facing a fiscal meltdown. Terrorists were trying new tricks. The southern border was turning into a Wild West Show where gun fights, drug smuggling, and illegal entries were common news headlines.

In order to carry out the heist from the federal treasury the Chicago banker with his sympathizers and lieutenants gradually built a powerful political base. He was taking control of political campaigns, stacking the deck in his favor. The need for a strong one-sided government was a necessity to pull off the caper, so he backed the campaigns of loyalists. Most of them were Democrats and their party ended up in control of the country. He used the unbalanced government to his advantage.

It was a well thought out plan. The vary top of the pyramid had to be like minded. To elect a socialist president he needed to court the vote of disgruntled Americans.

A block of voters went to the poles demanding change. Women, young whites, blacks, and Hispanics all contributed to the banker's scheme. The entire operation was conceived in South Chicago and it worked to perfection.

The banker, also known as the godfather, was a devil of a man. He directed his syndicate to crawl under the skin of political campaigns. Silently feeding the political coffers produced the intended results. Politicians, after being elected to office, sided with most of his requests. When more muscle was needed to enforce his demands he turned to union pressure or his lieutenants and even thugs if needed.

When foreign agents met with the godfather they saw the skill of a mastermind. He could tilt America's political stance. They wanted this man on their side.

Banking failures and housing foreclosures folded into the operation. These were necessary steps in the process. Make the people unhappy, but keep them returning to the government's safety net.

The easy part of the plan was allowing congress to spend freely on social programs. They want to stay in office, so they furnished the taxpayer dollars to keep programs funded.

With one party ruling the country the checks and balances of government were off the table. A greater effort was coming. It was going to push the heavily Democratic congress into making risky bets on healthcare, saving the economy and the environment.

The foreign agents found value in sinking America's businesses. Then they would make the products and cultivate the decline in America's industrial might.

Sounding the alarm bell, the mastermind whispered, "The world's financial system is about to collapse."

This was the beginning step of the Chicago banker's plan. Heard by government financial experts and passed along, a massive bailout easily passed through both houses of congress.

The ball was rolling. America's wealth was slipped away, like water pouring into the sewer. The bailout only added cheese to the trap. More give-a-ways were coming and foreign hands were extended. The presidents of America were unknowingly playing into the heist, but the new president became a victim to the love of power and adulation.

Like the Pied Piper of Hamelin, he played a tune for the poor. 'Spread the wealth' was the keynote phrase and part of the scheme. The president had one foot in the trap. He spoke the magic words. By keeping America's poor and unemployed happy, they would vote in the right direction and he would be admired for his compassion.

This played well for America's enemy. They would help to inspire one party rule. The possibility of insurrection, tyranny, and a takeover by the government was on the table.

Congress was playing into the game, blinded by their thirst for power. They instituted honorable programs in the name of righteousness. Each policy they produced was well crafted to aid the poor, the homeless, and the unemployed. The villains knew how to set the trap. Money spent keeping the unemployed, healthy, well fed, and lazy would undermine the country and agitate those who held good jobs.

Each new policy deepened the divide. The division included the illegal aliens crossing into America from Mexico. The taxpayer was footing an ever increasing bill and those receiving the gifts had no complaints. The gulf between the two was festering. It was only a matter of time before the unthinkable, the second civil war, revolution, or anarchy.

An unscrupulous banker was in charge of the plan. It was working. His background was rooted in corruption. He would continue work on the American side of the operation. The foreign figures would assemble and step in after all the pieces were put in place.

Anarchy might come sooner if the banker were both lucky and cunning at the same time.

Since the world financial market was teetering on bankruptcy, the timing of the plan was well conceived and the mood in America was feisty.

The long drawn out war made the voting public eager for change, but they never expected the president to be so radical.

When congress provided a fortune in taxpayer dollar for the banker to plunder, he knew the plan was working. With the government trying to keep track of the stimulus money it was like looking for a penny in the ocean. It meant millions would end up in the banker's pocket.

Too many Americans mistook the message 'spread the wealth' to mean a free ride from the government. What was being offered? It was a step to change America. A slow progression to socialism was coming to roost in society. .

Jobs disappeared. Many hard working Americans found distaste in giving away the fruits of labor to the taxman. That was the message in the promise. More criminals were slipping into Washington DC as if they were the offshoot of Al Capone regime.

The process may have looked orderly. Systematically, America's defenses were being torn down. Pledged rights were being given to the enemy. They had almost changed the face of the country. The seriousness of the situation wasn't fully realized until the treasury was milked beyond comprehension.

One of the first steps the new president made was to appoint czars to run the country. A major shift was taking place. The regime was ruling from the left.

Citizens started to doubt their choice. Questions were in everybody's mind. Would the change professed by the president work? Could America afford this kind of change? When would the recession end?

Chapter 3

BUSINESSES ARE HURTING

Palmino Franco saw the recession coming, but this recession was different. Military spending on war and terrorism had something to do with it. The real villain of the downturn was the government. They were spending money foolishly.

The downturn was being perpetuated by the people making the rules. They weren't business friendly, so businesses reduced staff and hunkered down.

Franco's Oregon businesses had to tighten their belts to stay alive. All across America it was the same. The economic crisis was national and it was accelerating. Once he understood their motive, he told his mistress it was time to fight back.

"Simone, I can't keep shedding workers to stay in business. Something is wrong with the way these people are ruling the country. Many people are being forced into bankruptcy. The president and his staff don't know much about business. The only fixes I hear - raise taxes and spend America's money on foolhardy programs.

Simone asks, "What about healthcare reform? Isn't that going to save; I mean, they said it'll reduce the cost of healthcare insurance."

Franco answers with a couple questions.

"Will insuring thirty million more uninsured Americans reduce your premium? Does the government ever spend money wisely? They're not trying to fix anything. They're lying. It's all about control."

Simone asks, "What are we going to do?"

Franco says, "I'm getting taxed to death here. It's time to go back to Ohio. We're going to keep building the sports complex out there. Maybe we can figure out how to make the casino a reality. If we pull out of this mess, sports and gambling are two sectors that'll recover."

On the political front Franco knew the country had taken the wrong path. They stacked the deck so heavily with one party that the country was almost a dictatorship.

It took a one-sided collection of political leaders to make changes. They were on course to change the republic.

Somebody sinister was running the opposition party. The kingpin was an underground boss with a variety of aliases. One of his many identities was Julius Jewels J. Cambello or Hades, god of the underground. Hades became regarded as a giant in the underworld because he knew how to manipulate United States politicians.

Julius found out how to entice a politician, simply use a campaign a campaign contribution to set the trap. It was like cheese to a mouse. He would often further the ruse by using coins or paper money, often times gold coins.

He would always start out by offering a fat contribution to their campaign. Once they got to know him the rest was easy. Offering to help a politician get into office was the first step in taking command of their vote. Money always worked.

Cambello's style would vary, but money was king. He often assumed control of political campaigns. It wasn't important to be a Republican or a Democrat, but one-sided control was the classic command structure.

Cambello only wanted them to vote for issues that increased his take. Starting out slowly over the early years, he got the right congressional members into office. With that being done it was easy to conjure up spending bills that would support his habit. That habit was spending other people's money for his benefit.

Party balance was ok, but it would never feed his bottom line like an unbalance political system. His successful management through recent elections earned him a major majority. The reason he like one party rule was understandable. They could push spending bills through congress without much haggling.

One of the purposes of Congress was to spend taxpayer's money for the good of the country and Cambello played this purpose well.

Making periodic visits with his lobbyists he became a friendly face to many political figures. One fact he knew so very well, they weren't good at spending money wisely.

Early in his financial career, Cambello went through some tough spots. He and Franco fought a few times over control of the family business. He was the big loser in the bitter dispute, but that was over ten years ago.

After escaping a mafia type war in Oregon, Julius went on to work his way into the Chicago banking system and amass a small banking fortune in Middle America. After taking control of several banks, he learned to include a few political figures to increase his fortune. The body of a godfather started to form through manipulation and corruption. His syndicate gained size to include a few media stations. He saw radio and TV as the method to advance his political agenda.

Although it was necessary to twist some arms once in a while, he was calm and collected most of the time. Dirty work was left up to lieutenants. Most definitely known for being a financial wizard, the Chicago elite and many politicians knew Jewels by his real name, Julius J. Cambello. Rarely would anyone see the middle name, Julie, on a document.

America found out she needed Mr. Cambello's advice because she was heavily in debt. He was there to advise which meant to stir the financial picture in his favor.

Because the people elected a relatively unknown and unqualified president, Cambello became even more important to the government.

The president had a social reform policy, which mirrored Cambello's idea and he used it his advantage. Greater financial rewards were ahead as congress dumped billions and billions of taxpayer dollars into the system. The perception he wanted the leadership to follow was simple. Julius wanted them to know he was at their service, secretly and unscrupulously he milked the treasury.

Politicians didn't know the extent of his travels. The places where he cultivated business ties were in Europe and the Middle East. That was a well kept secret.

When the recession hit the country square in the eye the national debt was high. Rising public debt was forcing congress to raise taxes. It was part of Cambello's plan. He instigated the issue by fanning the flame called change. This was the word Cambello put in the minds of the voters using his media outlets.

His three prong approach to taking control of government spending was through the media, banks, and politicians. He wanted his people in office in order to continue fleecing the treasury. He was already making tons of money in Chicago from various government programs.

Citizens saw the national debt from war as a sore spot. As the mood in the country soured, it was only natural for Cambello to set the trap. Playing up the evils of bad loans in the banking industry and Wall Street's dastardly deeds, he capitalized on the bad publicity.

By siding with the right politicians he placed himself in position to assume power and control. He was behind the scene directing the operation. Almost on cue and playing into his hand, voters wanted change in the political structure. By backing various political campaigns, Cambello helped to cause a super majority to be elected to both houses of congress. The right people were now organized. The next operation that was on the do list was to get congress to approve more spending.

All of this upheaval really forced the people to act without understanding the end result. Cambello, taking advantage of this situation, merely let the people elect a weak leader to run the country.

Mistake after mistake piled up because the president never ran a business and certainly not a country. Cambello sat back at the controls.

The next part of his plan was to remove trillions of taxpayer dollars from the United States Treasury. He was doing it bit by bit. It was all done under the disguise of saving the economy.

Cambello took advantage of the recession as more and more money was wasted on saving the economy. The damage to the economy appeared in the form of shuttered businesses, long unemployment lines, and more and more homeless.

Chapter 4
THE ROAD TO CHANGE

It took Julius Cambello over twelve years to set the stage for the second civil war. He owned a chapter in the book of Chicago politics. The first dark-skinned president, acting like a black knight, was about to seize power in the country. Half the country's citizens were ready for change and the other half had survival on their mind.

Though everything appeared rosy at first, the climate turned cool as congress forced one spending bill after another on the citizens. The king of the podium cried change, but sparks were flying nationally.

The change lit fuses across the country. One after another, Boston Tea Parties were forming. This wasn't by design, it developed as a people's revolution and even Cambello missed seeing the uprising.

It all started like a snowball rolling down the hill.

Americans were so bogged down by terrorism, wars in Iraq and Afghanistan and government spending, citizens wanted change. Panic overrode good judgment as they were will to try anything or any one to turn the country round.

Supporting the political machine running the country was a mobster. In the open his deeds were legal. His union lieutenants and his banks kept people in line. It was the slickest and most sinister operation ever put in place.

Mr. Cambello, through his Chicago banks and party affiliation, was gaining considerable respect from the ruling party. He was determined to expand his base of influence. A greater vision was to link his banking operation with the International Monetary Fund.

He got his wish. In no time he was hooked up with foreign leaders. His political acquaintances in Washington DC sent out an alert. 'Cambello can be trusted.'

He travelled to the Middle East to attract OPEC money. While visiting the Persian Gulf, he found more than he bargained for.

Diplomats introduced themselves as he stepped off the Kuwait Airways plane. United Arab Emirates officials ushered him to a limo where he was taken to a hotel. Everything seemed to be set up. He met more intriguing people.

When he eventually met with government officials, he was surprised they knew of his Chicago banking operation. One member of the fiefdom even suggested a meeting with an arms supplier. This sort of shocked him, because his arms dealing operation was somewhat of a secret.

It was clearly evident he was being recruited. He knew one of them had connections to al Qaeda, the terrorist organization. The sheik said so. The honesty was difficult to believe. If somebody was going to cause trouble in America, Cambello wanted to know before hand or at least get a heads up, so he warmed the relationship with the oil tycoon. He was introduced as Sheik Rayhan Omar Mahdi

There was plenty to talk about and Cambello didn't waste the opportunity. Inviting Sheik Mahdi to his south Chicago villa was a natural step. He accepted and a week later they were together in Chicago.

Cambello found out that the sheik had brothers in the United States. As their conversation drifted to banking he discovered the brothers were owners of a Detroit bank.

This was positive information because the government was about to lend a hand to Michigan. The American auto industry was facing some tough times. Poor sales, almost a crash of auto titans GM and Daimler Chrysler, put their stock on suicide watch. He wanted his bank to handle a big piece of the government bailout.

More and more information emerged as their discussion centered on gold, oil, and guns. This was right up the mobster's alley, although his satellite network handled this business and the illegal gambling business. His people could deal in weapons of all types. To reveal this secret so early in their initial meeting would have been caustic, so Cambello refrained and did most of the listening.

He gathered enough out of the talks to realize that Sheik Mahdi was involved with legal and probably illegal arms deals. The interesting part of the talk was that his brothers' Detroit bank was connected to the financial aspects of arms sales. The subject was dropped after a few minutes in favor of OPEC oil. In the back of his mind this arms business was another deal in the making.

Both Cambello and Sheik Mahdi knew oil was the life blood of America. Over the years America's politicians refused to let big oil look for the mother lode of oil which was in ANWR, the Arctic National Wildlife Refuge. They laughed about this because Mr. Mahdi and his friends were selling high priced crude to the United States. Mahdi told Cambello another laugher.

He says, "You know me as Sheik Rayhan Omar Mahdi, but I'm also called Road Oil by my Arab friends."

A smile broke across the sheik's face. It was a laughable name with petroleum as the reference. His name was contrived by the fact that one of his gushers created a road of oil. As he told the story their relationship cemented. As the sheik ended the story the conversation turned to a more serious subject.

Sheik Mahdi remarked, "The World Syndicate can always use a new member, who isn't afraid to make new friends in the Arab world."

Cambello didn't commit right away, thinking it might better to contact his Hungarian friend and discuss the matter. Nodding his head in apparent approval he let the sheik do the talking. They both knew about the World Syndicate.

Road Oil's friends had been doing business all over the world. These dynamos of world business had a common thread. They were all tied to the United Nations. They were profiteers. Profiteers in Sheik Mahdi's eyes meant the rich got richer. He let it be known that they had been feeding off America's war machine for a long time.

The world's money men, members of the World Syndicate, couldn't satisfy their greed. They put America under one strain after another.

Running up the price of oil and creating hot spots to fuel war was making them richer. The World Syndicate was selling arms to everyone to keep America's military busy. Their best trick was to keep the Palestinians feuding with Israel. Another ploy was using pirates to intercept shipping. This started a bit of a war between World Syndicate members, but it was another way to make an easy profit. The Somali pirates caused enough trouble to drag the French, British, Canadian, and American warships into the area off East Africa.

The little people, Somali mercenaries, were thought of as loose employees. Although they acted like mercenaries, the pirates and some terrorists got weapons and money from the World Syndicate. Any way the World Syndicate could keep America spending was doing their business justice. America always seemed to have a bottomless pit of money.

Road Oil pointed out that sending in teams of terrorists created plenty of havoc for Americans. This was all planned out he said.

The World Syndicate was a phrase to describe a world class criminal organization hell bent on profiting off Western civilization. Mainly they were made up of tycoons and dictators, who were truly world bandits. Titans of power described their hold on the world economy. Their holdings and empires were interwoven and reached around the globe. From Zurich, Switzerland to Chicago, Illinois they played a game of world monopoly with a religious backdrop.

Profiting from war, the World Syndicate didn't care too much about a winner. It was the organization that ultimately won, that is, until greed started to sap their power.

Mostly trusted names in the financial world, the World Syndicate ended up with a huge money problem. Because of their own devious character, they turned to cheating on each other.

Massive building projects in the Arab world ended up grossly over priced. The oil sheiks under cut the price of crude and over sold their OPEC limit. Arms dealers were being swindled by Chinese and North Korean manufacturers.

If it was a game between members of the World Syndicate, it ended when the world economy tanked. They caused far too much spending by the Western nations. The damage done to the world's economy was almost beyond repair. For one there was too much credit being shuffled around. The debt that was passed around expanded until it became a massive balloon. The world banking market was ready to burst.

The sheik told Cambello solving this problem would require the World Syndicate to extract more from America.

Cambello says, "Unfortunately sheik, America has a similar credit problem. She's borrowing and borrowing to satisfy her own debt."

He was referring to the long, expensive wars that the World Syndicate created, but he saw a perfect way to volunteer his banking services in the hopes of cashing in on both sides of the problem.

Cambello pointed out that America had other problems. Social programs were stripping the country's ability to borrow. The wealthiest nation in the world was living on massive overdrawn credit.

He says, "I'm on your side, sheik. The syndicate needs me. Let everyone know I'm a banking expert."

From that point on he made his way into the World Syndicate. The sheik departed with a clear understanding that Cambello would hear from the World Syndicate.

Trying to keep a lid on the boiling pot of world debt would require somebody getting burnt. The American taxpayer would have to carry the burden for the chefs, the American politicians.

At a hotel in Tunisia a meeting was held to discuss adding a new member to the World Syndicate, but he would have to prove himself. His temporary status was just the beginning. It didn't take long, Cambello moved quickly to become a member of the World Syndicate because of his multiple ties to American politics.

His people secured a footing with the United Nations. Bankrolling relief operations in North Africa and Haiti, donations were coming to his banks in all sizes.

That was a trademark of the banker. Cambello was where money moved and he earned a master's degree in governmental corruption. Members of the United Nations were perfect givers and takers. The members of the World Syndicate watched him operate. He was moving into foreign affairs as well as American politics.

When it was time to finance a campaign, he was there. When it was time to run a campaign, his sleazy tactics were the best. Doing anything necessary, his motive was to get the right people in there. He knew the political system. Being a great manipulator, he could buy into a campaign with ease. There was no doubt in the minds of the World Syndicate; he was behind some high political appointments.

His connection to the United Nations and foreign banks made him a key figure for the World Syndicate and it all started in Chicago. He was chosen to be the leader. An individual with his background would be able to fix American politics to favor the World Syndicate.

American politicians of both parties garnered votes by devising lavish spending bills. Cambello was making a fortune off their spending bills. It was easy to understand why. He was armed with insider information from both sides of the world. Politicians and the World Syndicate enjoyed doing business with the Chicago banker, Julius J. Cambello.

Chapter 5
THE TEA PARTY

The band was playing and American flags were waving in the air. A festival was in full swing. Something special happened in America. The mood changed and the feeling of patriotism swooped up half of America's citizens.

Palmino Franco, Simone Cooper, Richard Stern, and Brenda Clark made the Washington DC political rally a must visit. Standing in front of the bandstand, they listened to the speaker.

"What's wrong in America today?"

Plenty as the speaker would explain. The public debt was soaring. In America paying for social programs didn't seem to matter. Just print more money and borrow were the answers to the nation's problems.

Richard Stern whispers, "Keeping Social Security in the black is always put on the backburner. We have to start fixing these things. Hard times are here."

The speaker went on to mention that every time politicians added fresh programs to the menu the debt escalated. With no regard for paying the tab the situation was growing worse and worse.

The former Alaskan governor likened the situation to cooks in the kitchen. Both world debt and American debt sat on the stove side by side, one sizzling and the other steaming. As the kitchen grew hotter and hotter, the political cooks just stared at each other in wonder, not knowing what to do.

She says, "Their lack of action is typical Washington politics. If there are warning signs around, like 'Do not touch,' do not tax, do not steal, they aren't reading the messages. Americans can't afford this kind of government."

Stagnation and do nothing seemed to be the rule in Washington DC.

Finger pointing in all directions each political party didn't achieve much. The political process was out of control. The heat in the political kitchen was still rising.

The speaker pointed out that Americans of all races had been dining on the potpourri of social programs generated in the halls of congress without regard. Meaning, that is, without regard to who was doing the cooking and who was going to pay the bill. Congress didn't seem to care. It was always easy to pass the check around the table.

As the rally ended, the four Lake County, Ohio business people concluded that a new movement was really underway.

It was all starting to sink in. Realizing the depth of the problem, these Americans were starting to feel sick. It was time to send a message to congress. Tea Party folks stopped buying off the political menu as if they went on a diet.

They formed something new, a patriotic force. A revolutionary party started forming. Its job was to stop wasteful spending and think about saving America.

For the party in control this meant danger. Pet projects might be in danger. Something drastic had to be done to choke off the movement. The Democrat's answer was to shift the wealth as the leader declared. They thought a meat cleaver to the pay check of the upper middle class would get the job done. The cure, raising taxes, was the answer. It had a damaging effect on the economy, but still the tax structure was adjusted.

Some social programs would have to be modified. State budgets and America's society would have to change in order to share the wealth.

As the foursome was driving back to Ohio they talked about the speakers statements. One, stealing from the taxpayer was usually easy. Two, new programs weren't doing much good. The one program had a funny name, TARP Reform. It was a give-a-way program and congress was passing more spending bills.

Franco says, "Like the speaker said, 'The Stimulus Bill, bank bailouts, and loan modifications, they're putting it in the cooking pot of public debt.' That debt is going up and up."

Brenda Clark says, "When they passed Healthcare Reform, it was a signal. We're going to have some serious indigestion in this country."

Brenda knew about belt tightening from her work at the county commissioner's office. The county government had programs that were being reduced if not slashed to the bone to protect all the county residents.

A giant upset was definitely forming inside American. Stern and the others heard the burp at the Capitol. From coast to coast the noise was coming from the Tea Party. In Washington the press secretary called it Tea Party flatulence.

"The tea bags are just a lot of hot air."

Chapter 6

THE COMMITTEE ELECTS THE GODFATHER

The sea of greed was running deep throughout the world. In the grand scheme a plan was hatched to save the World Bank from collapse. The world banking system was straining. It started out as a rich man's chess game as large banks moved money around the world. The sweet deals unraveled.

Preying on each other, the bankers and insurance giants make dubious loans and guarantees. They become victims of their own shenanigans. The trail of graft ran from Asia to the Middle East and Europe. Sandwiched somewhere in the middle was the United States.

The United States Treasury had to be used as a giant bailout tool. Doing all the work to salvage the banking system was the American taxpayer. The people were the pawns in the game. The kings and queens occupied Washington DC.

Life for the poor had changed in America. A smorgasbord of safety nets was set up to capture any one with a problem. With so many programs to choose from the government had to set up one department after another to keep track of all the money used to finance the programs. For the time being most taxpayers went along with helping the poor, but this was becoming an out of control rollercoaster.

Every state in the union had programs. One for education, one for healthcare, children, seniors, drug addiction, etc., you name it, a program was out there for everyone.

The states that were most generous were the ones in the most trouble when the unemployment numbers started to rise. Generally, they were states run by Democrats.

The job market was closing in America. For those lucky enough to have good jobs, they strained to keep financial order. The taxpayer with a good job was a shrinking man or woman. The taxman was devouring the paycheck and gaining weight.

Too many people were losing out in the country. Home mortgage problems and credit card troubles forced many Americans into bankruptcy.

A great many con artists were coming to fix the problems. Too busy taking care of everyday activities many citizens mistook the crooked deals being arranged in Washington DC for an honest effort to save America from financial ruin.

The beginning of the end was started many years ago. Partially started by allowing the borders in America to be invasion routes, the visitors were really looking for a better life. Another malfeasance was allowing corporations to ship entire companies and the life blood of America, jobs, overseas. While it was paraded around as a way to expand the economy, it had serious consequences. By not building in America the country's work force shrank. Without as many taxpayers the money flowing into the treasury was diminishing.

To keep themselves in office politicians pumped out one social program after another. Americans didn't wake up in time to see what was happening. Congress didn't confront the consequences of the debt. At the same time the world financial market was falling apart. A congressional committee was playing lip service to the problem. Behind it all was the World Syndicate and their committee. They searched a bank database for a qualified candidate to fix the problem.

The sole duty of the committee was to pour over the computer records and hire a financial fireman. A financial expert was needed to find an answer to the banking mess. The database yielded one standout, but could he be trusted.

The computer scored the man high on financial matters, but low on integrity. He had a shaky background. After a whirlwind discussion it was decided.

The World Syndicate's committee decided that Washington politicians might be coached into throwing money at their problem and they would use the somewhat devious Washington insider, a Chicago man, to salvage the world's financial system. This is how Cambello became the financial kingpin.

The man they selected would have to come up with a rescue plan. The situation was so out of control they had to go with the Illinois banker.

A man of many titles, a Chicago banker, Hared Hades, aka Julius Cambello, alias the godfather, seemed like the perfect organizer. He was known to make political adjustments. He knew how to buy influence without raising suspicion. He was a master at rigging the vote. The committee agreed with the computer.

Julius and his syndicate were hired. They would be working for the committee, who were executive members of the World Syndicate. This was a big job for Julius. He knew the answer and used the opportunity to further his own ambition.

The timing was great. The left-wing people were in control. He decided their numbers were lopsided enough for the heist to work.

His men, an army of lieutenants, wore many hats. Attorneys, lobbyists, union chiefs, and thugs, were well connected to the political system. They could be called out as needed to fix problems.

The computer missed a small anomaly. It was Cambello's personal vendetta.

The godfather had a personal score to settle with a man in Ohio. It involved an old beef. It was one idiosyncrasy that made Julius a risky bet to fix the World Syndicate's problem.

Julius Cambello accepted the World Syndicate assignment, but in the back of his mind the small problem in Ohio troubled him the most. It had the potential to cause a string of horrific events.

Chapter 7

TRANSACTIONS

Julius got right to work.

Through a number of US banks, Julius arranged transactions. The deals had federal implications. Under the cover of a stimulus package taxpayer's money was moved around the world. It was the first of many steps that had to be made. With so many banks in trouble it was easy for his people to assemble special rescue accounts. The Troubled Asset Funds fit well in the scheme.

Incredible amounts of money were moved from bank to bank. His banks in Chicago used Troubled Asset Funds to acquire weaker banks. Shifting money, it was a white collar crime, but the funds were always repaid.

Extortion, when needed, was used against the banking executives and their family members. No banking executive wanted trouble if he or she was going to walk away with a clean reputation and a hefty bonus. Lastly, Cambello had the records expunged.

Over the years Julius had his close calls with federal officials. FBI and IRS agents had to be watched because Julius had trouble buying influence into these federal departments. This was one area he feared the most.

Loaned out money was nothing more than paper transactions. Getting his hands on large quantities of free cash was another matter. It involved building the illegal gambling trade. Sport's betting was big business in America. Through his banking network he bought into many bars, lotteries, race tracks, and a few casinos.

He needed huge amounts of taxpayer's money to solve the international banking problem. This would require fixing the political system. The focus would be on the politicians. They had to stay in office or be removed by his usual method, extortion.

Sex scandals and tax evasion were two of his best methods. He had the right girls or boys and the money to make it happen. Once he captured a politician's loyalty or threatened their reputation, he was in control.

Cash, silver, and gold coins worked well to steer the politician's vote. Gold coins were the favored barter. Cash was difficult to trace. Gold coins offered a special appeal. Politicians would feel good knowing they could acquire such rare beauty especially at a time when gold prices were skyrocketing.

All the godfather wanted was to buy the right influence.

Political campaigns using the right political flavor had to be organized and fixed. The godfather's team of activist worked on the national media. They would be used to carry the message.

To do this a lily white vision of change was commercialized. It was used to adjust the voter's thinking. Julius didn't see the mistake in the commercial for it turned into a political movement. The Tea Party movement started growing, but not all at once.

Change in America didn't sink in right away. For the general populous who went along for the ride they found out change meant trouble for the private sector. Most everyone was thinking that life would be better with a new man in charge. For awhile there was peace, but roiling in the belly of America was suspicion. Something wasn't quite right like a hissing sound under the hood of an auto.

The godfather was working in the halls of congress. His bribery tricked the weak. His lieutenants acted as messengers to remind those collecting the bounty that they owed their vote to the syndicate. Coins of influence floated around to ensure his programs got done. Many Americans cried foul. Like rubbing alcohol on a wound, Cambello's sleaze produced the cry.

The steamy voices of angry protesters started to appear. Faces of everyday people started to form brigades. They had plenty to say to the political figures walking up the steps of the Capitol. Both the politician and the people were almost out of control.

The real problem facing the nation was government spending. It created anger. The taxpayer was getting mad.

The country was being run by politicians that came out of Chicago. The godfather was in control of them.

Franco came to the realization that the country was being run by a biased personality. He wanted to succeed and beat back the government's misguided policies. He had to test his business smarts in Ohio.

Ohioans decided they wanted gambling. He knew the gambling business. To that end it didn't take long for Palmino Franco to find out how devious politics can be. In less than a month he was shafted by the political machine in Ohio when everything seemed to be in his favor.

He was watching the protesters on TV with Richard Stern. Other employees gathered at the business meeting. Franco asked the questions as Mr. Stern and the others listened.

"How deep is the corruption? Who's running this government?" asked the flamboyant entrepreneur.

His words were very much the same as those at the Capitol building in Washington DC. He voiced his opinion as a determined leader. It was time to join the opposition party. He and his employees would be part of the revolution.

Franco says, "We're going to fix America, not tear it down."

In a fascinating way the growing revolt was similar to the actions of the Boston Tea Party and General George Washington. The country was being scorched from bad government. Even Abe Lincoln founded the theme of honesty in government. When Abe was elected the first Republican president, he wanted people to be free of government control. A rising sentiment was building among Franco's staff.

Brenda Clark said, "Their not listening. High taxes and no representation is how it started, Mr. Franco. We're living the story of the Boston Tea Party. It's hard to believe. It's happening all over again."

They watched together. The mass of people were forming lines.

It was obvious one woman from Alaska was helping to form the new party. Her actions and those in her group were a lesson learned from the 1773 Boston Tea Party. It was a tax revolt. What Franco and his employees were seeing was the new revolutionary movement. It was truly a growing opposition party. It reflected the harsh feelings of resentment about the way the government was spending taxpayer money. All across America it was the same. Citizen groups were meeting and organizing to express frustration with government legislation.

There weren't many people around that could understand the 1929 Stock Market Crash. The stock market tumbled and the nation was adjusting to a new reality. The correlation wasn't quite the same, but high unemployment was the same. The government was trying to spend its way out of the trouble.

A clash was brewing. Greedy, corrupt politicians were running the country.

Events leading up to the Second Civil War had to do with civil rights. Freeing businesses and citizens from government control was the issue. Businesses were under attack. Citizens were becoming slaves of the government by relying on handouts.

Politicians didn't hide their mistakes. In your face corruption was accelerating to the point that the government acted as if it was king of the country. They were spending money without regard to the consequences.

Franco had the feeling that the government was trying to control the population through socialism. Half the citizens wanted to remain free of government controls. The other half of the population needed handouts. The results were starkly opposite.

The actions taking place in Washington, DC found the people taking to the streets. The Second Civil War was brewing.

Chapter 8
GOVERNMENT CORRUPTION

Palmino Franco had an idea to reverse the trend in Ohio. He went full speed ahead on an ambitious building project to make Northeast Ohio the sports capital of the country and a haven for spectators and tourists. If his Sports Park took off, he could provide many part time jobs and bring some good news to Ohio.

Franco took advantage of the hard times by buying land at rock bottom prices. Skilled laborers needed work. Many tradesmen were out of jobs, so he used them to build his sports complex.

The question facing Franco was a big one. Could the Sports Park stand on its own two legs in a recession that wasn't going away? Economists started using the phrase 'jobless recovery.' That didn't help matters.

State governments were burning through stimulus money. Tax refund checks were being withheld by some states to help shore up their money problems. This was a sign of the times. Using taxpayer money to keep states afloat instead of refunding money owed to responsible citizens who paid their taxes was almost criminal.

States were paying bills, but it was all credit, borrowed money. The federal government was printing money they didn't have. Prosperous states were exhausting their rainy day funds to pay unemployment benefits.

Franco and Stern had much to talk about as the newly built Sports Park was about to open. His casino part of the idea was off the table for the time being. It seemed to be a closed issue because of political shenanigans that prevented the Lake County casino from being on the Ohio ballot. Franco had a suspect in mind that dashed his casino hopes. That someone was out there.

Franco was never one to say never. He refused to give up.

Richard Stern says, "This president is running the risk of starting a national war." He was talking candidly to his millionaire boss. The country's citizens were deeply divided over many issues. Government spending, jobs and healthcare were the big ones.

Franco says, "Someone is either working with the president or has him out foxed. We can only hope the people stop this madness."

The Tea Party was calling for congressional action. It acted to encourage elected officials to listen to their demands. Town hall meetings grew, but the government became even more defiant. By passing legislation that wasn't supported by the majority of taxpayers, the ruling party thought they could force feed 'change' in America.

Palmino Franco says, "It sure looks like we're heading in the wrong direction. The government is changing, except it's changing for the worse. It's expanding and taking control of more and more personal affairs."

The tycoon was burned by his compulsive personality. He was trying hard to stay ahead of the government when he built his business, but government corruption had a hand in trumping his casino plan.

The owner of the newly built sports complex called Sports Park No. 1 was getting even more adamant about changing America back to normal. One third of the nation's citizens were barely getting by. Many were relying on subsidies in the form of food stamps, unemployment checks, welfare assistance, and countless other programs. It was becoming a way of life.

Franco asks, "Is this how it's going to be? We have more and more people on welfare, dependant on the government to make ends meet."

Franco and Richard were witnessing America on a down stroke and they didn't like it. Utility prices were rising. High energy prices had hit consumers and with no work it was tough to build consumer confidence. Those were just two of the demons making life painful. The bad news seemed to keep the misery ball rolling from state to state.

Home buyers who took advantage of ridiculous bank loans found out home don't always increase in value. The price of homes started to fall, mostly because of a political scheme dreamed up in Washington DC. Banks saw an army of people walking away from loans they should never have received. This had a ripple effect on the economy. A shockwave slammed the banking sector.

America's foreign wars gave voters a reason to look for new leadership. The knight with magic in his words rode into Washington after being groomed in Chicago.

Change was needed. The word 'change' was spoken as if it was an opening word to a mystical trance. The voters, thinking they were going to help the country by experimenting with someone new, found out different. His socialistic stance had a dividing effect on the country.

A new philosophy emerged. The federal government would take control of many businesses. Trouble for the country was shaping up.

Franco says, "Spread the wealth isn't going to work. People need jobs. Handouts will only fuel laziness. Work builds self-respect."

Franco and Stern watched large corporations reduce staff. Layoffs increased across all sectors of society. The downturn hit the home building industry and just about everyone. Usually the medical industry was immune from the belt tightening syndrome. The healthcare industry was the least affected, but their turn was coming. When the medical field started cutting back on nurses, it was a sure sign that the country was in a severe recession.

To add a measure of insult to doctors and nurses the president and congress made sure that professional group paid a price by ramming through a poorly constructed healthcare bill. The bill was another phony scheme to lower insurance premiums. The disguise was unmasked. The government wanted control of the medical industry. The bill was sure to degrade medical care and the doctors knew it.

Citizens watched banks fail. A general fear was taking hold. With the government stepping in to take control some large corporations no industry was safe. It was difficult to believe that American corporations, giants in auto manufacturing, were being taken over by the government.

The deficit spending issues were sounded by one administration and carried over to the new administration. Many politicians supported give-a-way programs that supplied taxpayer money to bailout big businesses that were deemed, 'to big to fail.'

As the housing market sank and sank, for sale signs littered the property across America. Homes and/or businesses were for sale on every street. For every business that was opening, two were failing.

A year into the recession employment tightened even further. This led to more home foreclosures. The signs of economic weakness were everywhere. Small businesses were usually the first to revive, but it wasn't happening.

Franco says, "Stern, if the president keeps separating the country into black, white, and Hispanic categories I'd have to say we've stepped back in history. He isn't doing much as a leader. The unemployed really face a hopeless situation if we don't start creating new private sector jobs."

Stern says, "We need a president, not a community organizer."

Franco adds, "I'm not taking any stimulus money. It's our job to make things happen without government help. The Sports Park has to be successful."

New and old words rang from the halls of congress. New stimulus programs and extended bailout programs were being concocted to save the economy. Franco would have none of it.

Franco says, "Stern, people are starting to ask questions. When is the stimulus going to work? How can they spend money they don't have?"

Stern says, "It's obvious, they didn't elect the right guy for the job."

The nation's leaders weren't adding jobs through the stimulus programs, but they kept touting recovery and saved jobs. The president was adding anxiety to a very apprehensive population.

When congress came up with healthcare reform, it was another nail in the coffin. Trouble with healthcare reform was easy to figure out. It didn't reduce healthcare premiums. It increased taxes to pay for the thirty million uninsured.

Franco made his disgust known by calling congressional delegates. Stern did the same. Together they had a feeling that the government might be doing all of this on purpose.

Franco questioned the actions of congress, "Are they in control or is the impossible happening?"

Stern asks, "What do you mean? Do you think a dictator is in the White House?"

Palmino Franco says, "We need an election before I say anything more."

What some well known media people seemed to be voicing was different from what the government was touting. Their voice had a major effect on the average citizen. Most people wanted jobs, not handouts.

The government stepped up with help, more unemployment checks were handed out. Because some states were running out of money, this did save jobs, government jobs.

They were the lucky ones. Others didn't make out. Private industry was paying the biggest price in this recession.

The big question was out there. Could the American economy be saved? The layoffs, closed factories, and shuttered businesses pointed to an America on wobbly knees. The nation was on the ropes and then it fell to a knee. A knockdown count was started.

Cambello didn't want the country to fail. His banking system was scooping up the government's money on all fronts. It was the Middle Eastern enemies, terrorists, and pirates that were working behind the scenes. They wanted oil prices to rise.

No one would rule out the possibility that a terrorist plot was used to strike another blow at America at a time when everything seemed to be going wrong. The oil rig explosion in the Gulf of Mexico was an environmental disaster. The timing of the event was certainly striking. The speed at which the government responded was slow for some ungodly reason. The administration seemed to be off guard.

At the same time Arizona citizens were up in arms from continuing illegal border crossings. People wondered if it wasn't all staged. Oil was washing up on the southern shore of Gulf States.

What else could go wrong? Hurricane season was right around the corner.

The government was facing an angry right-wing voter. Corruption was being murmured and politicians were being accused of cutting backroom deals and taking bribes. A couple of billboards asked questions. 'Do you miss me yet?' 'Are you only concerned with staying in office?'

The next election wasn't far away. To stay in power more leftists would be needed. New favors might be needed to keep politicians in office. Immigration reform was a way to sweep up millions of left-wing voters.

The country was again sharply divided over border security. States started to enact their own laws to reverse the government takeover. The Second Civil War was shaping up.

Chapter 9

THE PRO AND THE CON

The president and many of his socialist friends were forgetting about the Constitution. For the country and the citizens this was a huge mistake. It all seemed to be by design. America's enemies wanted the president to aggressively divide the blacks, Hispanics, and whites. The social disparity would feed anarchy resulting in the Second Civil War.

"What do you mean? Keep pushing the president," said Mr. Cambello.

Replying with a smile on his face, Sheik Rayhan Mahdi says, "He's having trouble quelling the anger on the streets. That's good."

The godfather was concerned about how far the terrorists were willing to go. It was the next elections that could work against him and change the course he set for the nation. He thought the worst. He might lose control of the Democratic Party. A majority of citizens were resolutely fixated on mending the nation's ills. The Tea Party movement was a big factor.

Reversing America's decline would require policy changes and it appeared that the Tea Party members were gaining an upper hand, although the government was running against the will of the people, they pressed forward.

Cambello believed Sheik Mahdi could on the one hand provide a boost for the administration. The president needed a small terrorist attack so the people would rush to the president's side. However, Cambello was concerned about the president's leadership skills. He could see the commander-in-chief was weak, almost ineffective when it came to taking charge of a crisis.

While the president and Cambello were having difficulties sorting out the nation's affairs, Franco found good fortune. The incredible was about to happened. Unexpected help was about to arrive that would change Mr. Franco's casino plans. Like a switch turning on a light bulb, a glow was about to remove the dark days, but the good luck switch could move in both directions.

Many experiences helped Palmino Franco shape his future. From the beginning the odyssey for Mr. Franco formed its roots in Painesville, Ohio where he went to high school. He moved to the West Coast after finishing college to seek his fortune.

In Oregon the business family he was working with had ties to the mob. He found himself wrapped up in the middle of a mini-war, a power struggle. The hotel business where he was working as senior manager expanded to include a casino run by the mafia. The business family fought with the mafia for control of the Oregon hotel and casino.

In less than a month the friendly atmosphere dissipated. A power struggle over the casino and hotel turned sour. Discussions got out of hand. The dispute turned violent.

What was a debate turned into a virtual brawl. Hand to hand combat escalated into a mafia gun battle. The battle took out the key players. This exchange wasn't the last, but it was hushed up to avoid a police investigation. Police did enter at the tail end of the conflict. At that point Franco gained control of the entire business almost by default. He ended up being the last man standing with enough knows how to buy the operation and turn the business into a mega-bucks enterprise.

The power struggle ended for Julius Cambello and his family of despots on the West Coast. It was a humbling defeat. In order to distance himself from Oregon he vanished from the scene and was actually thought to be dead. Some of Cambello's lieutenants went to jail. The group splintered for awhile.

Julius Cambello slipped away to Chicago to build an underground rackets business with a vow on his mind. He would even the score with Franco some day.

As time passed, Franco thought Cambello's organization disappeared. Both men became successful and wealthy.

In Chicago Julius reconstituted and took control of banks and the underground syndicate. His empire grew to include sports betting, gun running, and racetracks with multi-state connections. His lines of business grew.

For a period the banking industry was one growing enterprise. After many leaps, the housing crisis hit. The financial meltdown in the country put some banks out of business. Cambello swooped in to buy poorly run banks in Chicago and moved into Michigan, Indiana, Ohio, and New York.

His mafia connections were growing. Sport's betting was a huge money maker. His lieutenants were buying houses to establish new businesses.

His legal and illegal techniques were expanding. To foster and further a growing banking market political favors were bought. An understanding between politicians was established. They could all profit by loaning taxpayer money to 'save the local businesses.' This idea expanded to the federal government.

Initially, he persuaded congressional members to fund federal programs using taxpayer money (subsides) for the poor. This made buying a home affordable. Cambello's banks made a fortune writing risky loans. When the housing bubble burst, he bought the houses back for next to nothing. His lieutenants then turned some of them into professional stations for call girls and gambling houses.

His relationship with politicians worked like a Swiss clock. All it took was campaign donations. Politicians bent over backwards for the bankers support. Like a sponge, Cambello soaked up political friends.

He carried an air of charm around Chicago. Neighbors and friends thought the world of him, although his lieutenants knew the real character under the smiling face was a ruthless bloodsucker.

Palmino Franco spread his business wisdom in Ohio. By believing he could build a large sports complex even under the harshest of economic times. Included in the plan was a hotel and casino. He saw hope for Ohio and the nation. Building in a down market seemed like the right thing to do. He felt at some point the extreme recession had to subside.

What seemed strange to Franco was the unemployment picture.

It was hanging like August humidity in Texas. According to Franco, the government was causing the downturn and the unemployment, although he didn't want to assume their motive was dishonest. He thought it was the misguided idea of 'spreading the wealth.'

Franco's lofty plans included a baseball park with a track. The hotel and a casino, if he could get the Ohio State legislature to change the rules on casino gambling, would complement each other. For the Sports Park to really succeed the chief money maker, the casino, would need to open next to the grounds of his sports complex. If it didn't he would have to pay for the entire complex out of his own pocket. That would be risky as it would be a major drain on his wealth.

This money issue with Franco wasn't a well kept secret. Getting wind of the Northern Ohio Sports Park was Julius Cambello. When he found out Franco was masterminding the building project, which included a casino, he became jealous and angry. Immediately, revenge was on his mind. He had to do some damage, inflict some pain on his old adversary.

Through some careful political maneuvering, it was Julius, the godfather, who succeeded in tripping up Franco's casino plan using cutthroat politics to shutoff the idea of a Painesville Township casino.

He had his people in Ohio keeping track of the building project. Franco didn't quit on the complex, but this only stoked Julius' anger. When the time was right, he would snatch the park project from Franco, just like Franco did to him in Oregon.

Even though Julius Cambello amassed power in Illinois and surrounding states, he wanted more power and wealth. After over ten year of seething on the sideline he saw his chance to shaft Franco.

To get even would end his nightmare. Securing the title to the Sports Park would be the ultimate retribution. The hurt from the disappointing loss of the Oregon casino was a personal blemish on his Italian soul. If it all worked out, stealing Franco's Sports Park would certainly be a nice addition to his holdings and would calm ten years of anger.

He remarked about his anxiety to his portly lieutenant.

"Boris, I get even. Nobody gets away by crossing me. If they try, I will beat them. You remember this. I like to win no matter how long it takes. I don't care how I do it."

Boris says, "We know that, boss."

Chapter 10

JOB NO. 1

Julius had to wait for the right time to move in on Franco's operation. Another affair took center stage. The World Syndicate job was becoming untidy. At Cambello's urging, the International Monetary Fund loaned billions to Greece. Because of European socialism many countries on the continent were in financial danger.

Cambello stepped ahead of the pack to offer the leaders some sobering news. They would have to cut back on social programs and raise taxes. Mr. Cambello was worried he wouldn't see anymore kickbacks since the money supply was drying up.

Some of Europe's problems seemed to be under control after the IMF bailout, but Greece, Portugal, and Spain still had major financial problems.

Mr. Cambello decided to let the world markets settle. The U. S. Federal Reserve already loaned a bundle. His bank made out on the deal as usual. They received transaction fees and interest payments, so he could afford to let the European Union work with Greece. His partner, George Budapest, had his nose close to the deal. They could handle the Greek mess.

The godfather didn't limit himself to one business over another. By focusing on an array of enterprises he captured profits in many directions.

He spoke words of wisdom, 'Capitalism makes America a great

country, but socialism makes me rich.' which is how he looked at swindling the taxpayer.

His syndicate was a principal dealer in guns, ammunition, and explosives. It was a lucrative underground trade. With two different organizations asking for arms the business was heating up. It was becoming a front-burner issue when most businesses were sinking. The Mexican cartels wanted automatic weapons and some Middle Eastern groups were looking for guns and explosives.

In one instance the syndicate made a nice profit in Mexico without any bloodshed. A large weapons transaction was being formulated on the southern border of the United States. A takeover between cartels was brewing between rival gangs. If the battle stayed in Mexico that would be good, however, Cambello heard Arizona was feeling the effects of the power struggle. He intervened.

Using his middlemen and instigators, Cambello fanned the fire by sending his instigators to both camps. He didn't want to miss out on a big arms sale. Flying over the border in small planes, his Mexican lieutenants made friends with gang members in exchange for transferring illegal aliens to America.

They had automatic weapons on board for sale. They were scurrying to each camp on the Mexican side of the border. Their mission ended in success. Weapons were sold to both sides for a hefty profit. Julius didn't have to lift a finger.

Cambello knew Middle East terrorists were working with Sheik Mahdi on something. When Mahdi stopped at Cambello's estate to ask for guns, he thought another battle was brewing. Mahdi was pushing the godfather to sell weapons to his Pakistani friends in Detroit.

Detroit was a city in cardiac arrest and it had a large Muslim population. Cambello thought that the blacks and Muslims might be fighting against the growing Mexican population.

Sheik Rayman Mahdi told him the World Syndicate's financial problems were almost over. His statement wasn't true. This was a lie, something that Julius silently wondered. How could he say that?

Something seemed to be out of order. The World Syndicate's credit problem wasn't fixed. Mahdi was hiding something. Abruptly, Mahdi changed the subject and started talking about a Great Lakes venture.

Mahdi says, "I didn't tell you. We're working on a Great Lakes cruise ship."

Julius says, "That's nice, you'll take me for a cruise some day."

Mahdi adds, "No, you won't like this ship. We're moving people that are looking for a new life. Let's leave it at that."

Julius understood this to mean they were moving people illegally. After the men finished talking about the cruise ship, he was concerned. Maybe the idea was to transfer terrorists or illegal aliens from Canada to the United States or from the U.S. to Canada. Lake Erie and Lake Michigan ports were mentioned. Small ports wouldn't attract much attention. Cambello thought he must have misunderstood, but made a mental note of the discussion.

The cruise ship idea didn't fit Mahdi's profile. He was a member of the World Syndicate. He was hardly the type of man to be concerned about illegal immigration.

If Mahdi wanted him to stop work on the World Syndicate job, it was perfect timing. Julius had Palmino Franco on his mind. He was tormented by revenge. It was almost driving him to act irrationally. Julius wanted to drop everything and get Franco. His gut churning desire to get even with Franco was more important than anything else.

The Great Lakes cruise ship was a subject that fell by the wayside as both men seemed to be thinking of other things; that is, until Mahdi finished the meeting by saying something of a warning.

Sheik Mahdi said, "I'll get back to you before anything happens. You'll know in advance. Goodbye, I wish you well."

He walked out.

The conversation was strange. Cambello couldn't help thinking that Mahdi and his terrorist friends might be planning a hit in the Great Lakes Region or somewhere in the United States. A terrorist had already tried to blow up Time Square.

Julius turned the TV news on after Mahdi left. The president was talking away from the podium. Julius shook his head and pointed at the TV screen.

"Your success is because of me. I'm the leader. Mr. President, you are a fish out of water. You know nothing about financial matters or running a country."

Knowing he had other pressing matters that needed his attention, he finished by yelling at the TV screen.

"Keep it up, el presidente. You got the whole country twisted in a knot, but I'm wringing the dollars from your ineptitude. Don't worry, Mr. President, I'm backing you all the way to the bank. Ha ha ha!"

The president's timely wave was greeted with a push of the remote control. Off he goes as darkness settles on the TV screen.

Julius says, "Just don't start a civil war." That was on Julius's mind.

Chapter 11
JOB NO. 2

Franco's Ohio Sports Park was somewhat of a millstone around his neck. He was worried the money to keep building the operation would be slow in coming. Without a local casino to finance the operation it would be like buying a car without a job, but he was a gambler and a man who knew when to take chances.

On the other side was the godfather. His illegal gambling operation was doing well. With Franco opening up a Sports Park in Ohio Cambello's personality wouldn't allow him to pass up the opportunity to get even.

Cambello's behavior at this point was cool and collected while speaking to his men, but he was a live wire inside. Seething over the past, both Franco and he had skeletons in their closets. They were leaders of men for opposite reasons, good and bad.

Prioritizing problems sometimes confounded both men. Cambello was devoting more time to Franco's operation. Franco was wasting time on the casino issue. Cambello should have been steering the president's men away from making bad decisions on the economy.

He found out that the president's men and the people running congress were tripping on every step without his help. This had him a little concerned. The Tea Party movement was building support from all the missteps being made.

Speaking to his lieutenants he raises the concern.

"We've done well so far. A couple things are showing up that might set us back."

Paul Beach says, "What's the problem, boss?"

The godfather replies, "The Tea Party movement is growing.

"We'll be taking over some new businesses. Beaner, do you know anything about sports besides gambling?"

"Oh, yeah! I was a high school jock." Paul Beach replies.

"Well, never mind for now. Soon, I'm going to be the owner of a Sports Park."

With the World Syndicate's problem off the table Cambello could use some of the bailout money for his own Chicago projects. The money was just sitting in his bank. He wasn't making any loans. He was buying up bad loans with the taxpayer's money. Property was for sale everywhere and some big newspaper businesses were about to fold. He could almost bid on any business. His financial situation was too good to be true.

He kept his people busy buying arms and gold. In fact he was worried the bad times for the country would end. People were selling property, jewelry, and guns. The plunder was building. So much booty was coming to his collection center he had to build a second and third warehouse.

Gold and silver was the perfect commodity since the world's financial picture was gloomy. Making the best of the situation was most important. He explained the next political phase to his lawyer.

"Mr. Culliver, the president is doing everything right for us. We made a fortune on this guy. This was one of the best runs I ever had, but I'm afraid the people are going to turn on him, even his liberal friends. I can't keep this congress together. They're getting as greedy as me. The people are starting to wise up."

Mr. Culliver says, "Talk radio and the cable news people are laying the tracks for a return to normal. You better quit while you're ahead."

That was good advice which the godfather ignored. Signs of trouble appear as Mr. Culliver predicted.

Federal stimulus contracts had a tougher time marching through the banking system. Cambello's arms dealers south of Arizona got bogged down by that state. Arizona was getting tough about border security.

The general mood in the country was changing. The hurry to take advantage of the good times spelled trouble. Doing two things at once caused mistakes. Julius had a tendency to hurry. This caused slip ups.

Money had to be moved around. He had sacks of gold moving by armored cars. Cambello owned some of the fleet that moved the money. The cargo that moved was on manifests along with dates and destinations. This information left a footprint.

The godfather didn't mind using some of the gold to pay for favors. Political payoffs were common in Chicago politics. Hasty arrangements led to poor record keeping. Julius sometimes interfered with the record keeping. When Julius boldly maneuvered contracts, the FBI almost caught up to him.

A political squealer reported that bank president Julius Cambello viewed sealed bids and two politicians were caught changing numbers in the public contracts.

At that point a female FBI agent almost had him cornered, but a couple of Chicago politicians fixed the contracts. They were rewarded with cash to cover the mischievousness. Still, she was zeroing in on the culprits. The corrupt individuals were getting cold feet and told the ringleader the name of the squealer.

Mysteriously, all the men died together in an alcohol related auto accident before she could take their statements. The indictment went nowhere and the contract scam died with them. Nothing was ever proven and the case was thrown out. However, it was a sign of trouble for Cambello.

That was Julius' first brush with FBI Agent Monica Micovich. At that time she was a bloodhound and Cambello's tracks were leading up the political ladder.

From that contact Agent Micovich had a file on Julius Cambello, but not enough to tie him to rigging public contracts or paying for political favors. She was removed from his case since she was expecting her first child. The file was buried under more pressing issues.

Cambello was a cagy businessman. He always got away while other associates didn't fare so well. Micovich's work earned her a degree of notice with the godfather.

The godfather told his lieutenants, "You guys stay away from the Cleveland agent. The bitch was in Detroit and came to Chicago for some reason. She's trouble. When and if I get a chance, I'll take care of her."

The Cleveland, Chicago and Detroit syndicate members received news of Agent Micovich's deeds. They were put on alert.

Without telling her superiors Agent Micovich was gathering information on a far reaching case after learning about Mr. Cambello's political work. It appeared to have everything, corruption, political scheming, and possible embezzlement.

It was difficult to prove. Paying for votes was a huge scandal, if it could be substantiated. The corruption puzzle with many political leaders would surely shake up the nation. She couldn't be certain how far up it ran, but it seemed to start in Chicago. She didn't want to jump the gun. Many pieces still had to be assembled.

The case had a degree of danger. She didn't want to say much because she knew her supervisor would take her off the case because she was pregnant. She mentioned to Supervisor Cliff Moses that she was on to something big.

He abruptly removed her from the case because he was following orders.

Moses wouldn't tell her anything more.

Cambello had many connections to high government officials especially in the banking sector. He was helpful with resolving banking issues, although his motive was tainted by his connection to organized crime. He made friends fast. There was an adage in the banking industry. 'Make friends with rich people because the money rubs off.' It worked both ways for the godfather.

Nearly everyone considered him a generous socialite, who was unafraid to be labeled a left leaning environmentalist. It was difficult for him to remember everyone's name who received gifts. One person he wished to forget was Monica Micovich.

Agent Micovich sensed the mafia connections. Cambello had made friends with some dark figures. She relied on stakeouts and personal observations. That was in her final report, which was sanitized by someone. In the final report her supervisor added a footnote before he passed it along.

Due to the fact that Agent Micovich was approaching the third trimester of her pregnancy she was replaced by Agent Paula Gavalia. Agent Gavalia won't return to this investigation until she speaks with...

Supervisor Moses never finished the footnote.

Since Cambello was well connected to Chicago and Washington DC political leaders, he had an impressive list of personal references.

Any case against Cambello would need solid proof of his connection to organized crime. There wasn't rock solid evidence to tie him to organized crime, payoffs, or political blackmail.

With homeland terrorism rising on the scale manpower shortages led to a lapse in procedure and the case was nearly forgotten. Supervisor Moses was up to his eyeballs in work. Casino gambling was coming to Ohio and that created a new element to watch.

Julius Cambello wasn't just any ordinary executive. He was a multi-task dynamo. He was the ultimate schemer, a Cadillac of crooks. He knew who to pay, how to pay for political help, and when to collect the benefits.

Besides banking he used his companies, Media Empire, a cable TV business and newspapers to heap praise on politicians. The reason was simple. Great cooperation would grow. Political favors between unions, banks, Chicago businesses, and politicians meant profits would feed the bottom line.

When Cambello made the news in Chicago, Palmino Franco saw his face on TV. It was a day of reckoning. He knew the two would meet again. Franco already had an inkling his group was facing big time hitters.

During a conversation with one of his employees, Franco talked about the past. Richard Stern and Franco both faced some tough guys in their youthful days.

Reminding Stern of trouble Franco says, "You and Brenda almost bought the farm. I can't ask you and her to stay with me."

Richard says, "Hold on! I'm with you. Brenda Clark is a department head with the county. We don't need her."

Franco says, "I'll let her decide."

Franco didn't want to alarm his staff, but he knew how ruthless Cambello could be. Cambello and his men were almost certain to be watching the Ohio operation.

It was true. Julius Cambello kept a watch on the Oregon casino owner and his operation. When he found out Franco was trying to secure a casino opportunity in Ohio, he made some phone calls. The godfather had political clout. In order to prevent the Franco casino initiative from getting on the ballot for a citizen's vote, he resorted to his old tactics. He paid off the right people.

It was a major setback for the Oregon casino owner, but that didn't stop Palmino Franco. He had financial stability and a flexible plan. In his mind nothing was going to prevent him from opening his Sports Park. He would deal with the casino part of the plan at a latter day. For the time being he would have to learn how the enemy operates and take whatever defensive actions needed.

While the land base casino idea didn't succeed, a waterborne enterprise was still a possibility. Lighthouses on Lake Erie had always fascinated Franco. Fairport Harbor had an old structure that was on a list of lighthouses to be auctioned off. The next owner might use it as a summertime landing zone for casino boats sailing around Lake Erie. It might serve as a museum or photo stop.

His land based casino project on the shore of Lake Erie might be opened if he could get the people to vote on another casino initiative. That would have to happen down the road after the Sports Park becomes popular. The massive indoor dock he built would store casino ferries in the winter and use them in the summertime for gambling junkets to Canada. He had many ideas.

If all went well a new lighthouse restaurant could be built on the last portion of Water Street to complement the old Second Street lighthouse. At the end of the Mentor Headlands State Park a boardwalk to the west breakwater lighthouse could be built to accommodate fishermen, hikers, and tourists.

Six to eight months out of the year the operation could function. The state needed jobs and this tourist attraction would supply quite a few. The summertime setting was perfect. Boating, fishing, and river boat gambling on Lake Erie and maybe Grand River would bring Northeast Ohio back to life. The entire wharf from Willoughby/Eastlake to Mentor/Fairport Harbor and Perry/Madison would add to the excitement of a Water World and Sports Park.

Through Richard Stern's suggestion Franco bought into the idea of a Sports Park. The first project was paid for using Franco's casino fortune. The plan kind of mushroomed. The first portion of the Sports Park was built. Ohioans were voting on a casino gambling issue so Franco decided to build a hotel with a casino in the event he could secure a license to operate a casino down the road.

The hotel, casino, and Sports Park had attracted attention alright. Cambello's men were watching it all happen.

Much had taken place to lure Mr. Franco to Ohio. His Oregon casino was booming and he was flush with cash.

Before all of Franco's good fortune, a progression of events started the ball rolling. A national crisis was the first event.

Right after the turn of the century the nation had to face a sneaky, shadowy enemy called el Qaeda. The terrorist group wanted to damage the country's image. The jihadist planned a sinister attack. Terror from the sky was the tactic. Hijackers commandeered airplanes and flew the planes into the World Trade Center and the Pentagon.

The shock of it all sent the nation into code red. It was hard to believe; America was under attack. The suicide attack and murderers, who found a way to remain undetected, pulled off an unprecedented sneak attack. It started a protracted war.

It was a religious war, although many refused to call it that way. Radical Muslims were fighting a Western Christian civilization. A modern day crusade was the result.

America armed itself to thwart an enemy that had no national origin. The enemy was using terrorism, a warfare tactic, to confront America. From that day, September 11th 2001, America was on a war footing. It changed aviation freedom.

The FBI responded to the homeland attack. An investigation revealed details of the plot. The price tag to combat terrorism was enormous. Huge sums of money were spent to organize a defense of the nation. The Department of Homeland Security was formed. Border security was tightened. Months later the Afghan War started.

As time passed the infamous attack was filed away by many Americans. They were warned at the time that fighting terrorism would be a prolonged fight. As the years ticked by the memory of 911 faded.

The fact that the nation was forgetting about the World Trade Center attack was disturbing and sad to Richard Stern and Palmino Franco.

The two men were brought together by a letter to Franco suggesting Painesville Township in Ohio would be an excellent place to build a Sports Park and casino. It could be the centerpiece to Mid American tourism since Ohio didn't have casino gambling. Franco liked the idea. It was all happening at a time when the country was transitioning.

Chapter 12
AMERICA'S ENEMIES

America was truly changing. History was being made in America on another front. A new leader was busy exchanging private enterprise for socialism.

Campaign promises made good sense to many and many people thought they elected a black president.

The period of time split the nation's citizens into separate parts. The poor were all for social change. Those citizens without healthcare were all for a new government program. The unemployed wanted more and more help. The people without jobs seemed to be a special group because their numbers were growing into the tens of millions.

Many well educated economists warned that the country wasn't ready for radical change, even liberal thinking men and women joined the chorus.

The rich warned of high unemployment if the course for America was socialism.

The new president was pushing forward with an ambitious domestic agenda. The Tea Party was pushing back because they knew the government had no money to pay for social reform.

The last three presidents had left him with plenty of unfinished business and he wasn't ready for the job. Terrorism started rising under his feet when they saw his weakness. A one-sided congress was shirking their duties. They did nothing to resolve plight of the Social Security Trust Fund. Border security was still a problem.

Entitlements and free government programs carried a high price tag. Julius Cambello seemed to care about the borrowing except he was instigating and cheering for more programs. His syndicate was making out just fine.

A battle loomed between Democrats and Republicans. That was politics. The challenge facing the nation was to confront a housing crisis and record unemployment. The president and congress agreed on a solution, more spending. All of this social turmoil and the war in Afghanistan would take time to resolve. In the meantime the Tea Party was calling out congressional leaders to speak at public forums.

The clock was ticking on a divided public.

Richard Stern sat in his easy chair with his cats at his side. While cleaning his Remington 12 gauge shotgun as if he expected trouble, Stern clicked on the TV. His friend, Mr. West, had just sold him the gun. Cleaning it was the second to the last order of business before he had to umpire a Riverside junior varsity baseball game.

Mr. West's brother, John West, had a scope mounted 30/30 high powered rifle that he wanted to see and buy in the near future before the government outlawed gun ownership. As he sat there watching the news, he talked to the cats as if they cared.

"After eight year of war in Iraq, the public has spent enough. Billions and billions of dollars on the war, but we won. Freedom is costly, I pray for the dead and wound.

"Just when do we get our money back? Send us some free oil, Iraq. Look cats, now it's on to Afghanistan. What's in Afghanistan? The president fires his Afghan general and hires a G. W. general that he doesn't like. This country is in trouble with this president running the show."

A Second Civil War was really on his mind. Stern knew the country was fighting terrorism over there to prevent it from spreading. There were con artists driving America into a hole. Irrational thinking and greed were the drivers.

The president wanted to take from the rich and give to the poor. People poured across the borders that weren't protected. There were politicians running the country that only cared about their party and buying votes to stay in office.

Stern says, "Don't let any more terrorists and criminals come to America. I'll be ready. Shotguns are better for house to house fighting."

Richard answered the cell phone ringing at his side. It was his friend, Dave Skytta, down the street.

Stern says, "Hi Dave, I'm busy yelling at the TV. I won't go along with all these changes. The economy is dead. That's the problem. We can't afford all these changes. We're in a depression and the president won't admit it. He's tearing this country apart!"

Dave says, "Take it easy. You need to get to an AA meeting, buddy."

Stern wondered if the Tea Party movement could turn things around. Dave tried to calm him down and did for a second until he saw the Majority Leader and Speaker of the House on TV.

"We have to vote these guys out, Dave, and I mean the president and all his corrupt friends. They don't give a damn about the middle class. I'm going to the next Tea Party rally. That's where the sane people go now-a-days."

Stern knew he was right. The Tea Party folks were joining with Republicans and millions of disillusioned Americans. The big mistake was turning to a hapless president with false hope and phony change. The leaders only got in office because of the war and lies about change.

Dave says, "Just called to say hello. Catlin stopped by for coffee. Come on over before you blow a gasket."

Dave ended the conversation with his usual comment, "Thanks for being part of my life."

Richard says, "OK, Dave, I'm still sober. One of these days I'll stop, goodbye."

Stern resumed the cleaning process. He remembered Mrs. Urbanski's friend, Roger, a retired truck driver, telling him how easy it is to get a drivers license in the country.

Stern tells one of his cats, "Boots, we have to stop the southern invasion. This is one of many reasons the country is broke. We need a national ID program to make sure a person is in this country legally. If the government can take a census, a person should be required to show proof of citizenship."

On top of all the lies Stern was hearing on TV, the Speaker of the House talked down to the Tea Party people. She kept saying the stimulus is working and ignoring the rising unemployment picture.

"You lie, he lies, when will it end?"

Stern clicked the off button on the remote and turned on the radio.

With so much distasteful news surrounding the nation, it was impossible to predict how the citizens would handle another major terrorist attack. There were signs that another attack was coming.

The politics in Washington was dividing the country. People wondered who was running the country. Cambello knew. He was holding the puppet's strings.

Politics was constantly the subject on talk radio and TV. Some talk show hosts claimed they could see an evil empire building. Rush was on. It was one station whose ratings were going through the roof. It was obvious many people believed in the host.

The political leadership was riding around the streets in Washington DC like Roman emperors. The government was out of balance One party was ruling the country rather than governing the country. Battle lines were being drawn.

Journalism took on two distinct flavors. One group was a willing accomplice pushing the White House theme, spinning good news out of thin air. The economic forecast didn't add up to positive change. Yet, the stories heaped praise on the ruler for bringing the country back from the brink. Some journalists were shills, creating good news for the White House. On the other side there were right-wing journalists. They served to temper the tunes coming out of Washington DC. Trusting anything said about politics and global warming was a gamble for the independent minded citizen.

The drum beat coming from many Tea Party events painted a picture of an administration in disarray. The Tea Party had a message for voters. 'If you want to take back America, you'll have to vote the current leadership out of office.'

On the White House side of the street were the inline subjects, where a government job was fine. Their message was ambiguous. 'Stick with us it should get better down the road, but don't count on a solid recovery in the near future.'

Behind the scenes were powerful money men. They voted for the president, but started having second thoughts about the way the country was heading.

The public couldn't see Cambello's manipulation, political bank rolling, backroom deals, and the gift giving. Those operations were carried out in private.

Politics was on Franco's mind as he and Stern talked about the feud between the Republicans and the Democrats. Franco had a running battle with the mafia. He ran into the mob when he fought with them for control of the Oregon casino. He was the last man standing after arrests and several murders took out the warring parties. From that lesson in watching the mob operate Franco felt he was ready for a battle in Ohio.

What was unfortunate for Franco was the fact that he didn't want any part of politics. He didn't play the game. His opportunity to open a casino in Ohio was mostly wasted because of this.

Politician made promises to keep him guessing about his chances of opening a casino. He used a local business manager to work a deal in Columbus. She had sex appeal and worked from the podium like no other. She was fooled in the end.

Ohio politics was turning a corner. The people did decide on casinos for the state. Franco didn't receive government permission to operate a casino. The shutout was caused by the godfather. The man had control of people in Columbus.

A lesson was learned.

Franco says, "The people have no idea how bad things can get. The mob can pay off the right people. This can go on all the way to the top. That's what happened to us. I'm sure of it."

Franco was obviously disappointed.

Franco and Stern's friendship was building. They were two dissimilar men if their wealth was measured. One was super rich because of his Oregon hotel and casino and Stern was just lucky. He got to know some pretty good FBI agents along the way.

Profiling the enemy led him to distressful moments. He was lucky to be alive. The amateur bounty hunter and informer found meddling to be profitable, but the contagion to be lucky was stretched to the limit. Where he shouldn't go, Stern went.

Chapter 13
SMALL BUSINESS

His work at the presidential podium carried the power of a minstrel. Entertainment seemed to be the order of business rather than governing the country. Running the country seemed to be a secondary issue. To stay in power he needed to juggle the numbers. Deficit spending and unemployment was running through the roof.

Cambello told the presidential advisor the bad news.

Cambello says, "Europe is falling apart. Tell the president he has to keep hope alive. Just say it. Hope has to be repeated over and over. Make the people think he has everything under control. Tell the president to keep saying we're working to restore order, we're back from the brink, but it's going to take time."

The press secretary, sitting off to the side, was a little sick. The reporters and journalist were becoming less cooperative. Their questions were starting to zero in on the president's weaknesses. Newspaper articles wrote unflattering sentences.

He was turning into an empty suit. He's a bobble head doll with no real answers.

The press secretary says, "The president has many issues to contend with right now. We've inherited a mess. The president hopes we'll see the light at the end of the tunnel as the stimulus takes hold. Change for the better is coming."

Watching the dribble on TV was Cambello. He was the cheerleader.

Cambello replies, "Yes, I know. Just keep him talking up the hope and change. The blame game isn't going to work any more.

"The economy better get better or we'll end up with a second civil war."

Cambello didn't care that much. Gold prices were rising. He saw his chance to work another miracle. He was set to make another bundle by shipping guns to Europe.

Cambello tells the presidential advisor, "Have him call the German chancellor. She needs to hear some good news. We'll have the Federal Reserve send more bailout money. She doesn't have to worry."

The great orator called the chancellor. An agreement was reached. She would carry his message to the European Union and the IMF. Even though Mr. Mahdi said everything was stable in Europe, Cambello instinctively knew he was lying. Mr. Mahdi wasn't on the same page. This had Cambello thinking the whole process over.

He told his lieutenants to watch for bigger arms purchases. The guns will go to Europe, but might end up in the United States.

"Sheik Mahdi is up to something. The Great Lakes cruise ship is something to watch. He isn't telling all. His Muslim brothers in Detroit might be buying or receiving weapons soon. If they do, you let me know."

Europe needed bailout money too and it was a perfect time to continue the game of spending the taxpayer's money. The game had the government printing press running in overtime. Producing legal tender was robbing the treasury and forestalling the day of reckoning, but it was driving up the price of gold.

America's leader was more than a bit short sighted. His gauge of economics was slim at best. On the other hand his political thinking was pretty good. He was keeping the country divided in two, mostly whites on one side. The blacks were almost one hundred percent behind the president.

For Cambello this was good. Overall he knew the president really didn't have much time to prepare for such a big job. The president never had a private sector job and looking back further, he was always moving around.

During a portion of his childhood the president was raised in a

Muslim country and bounced around the world. Chicago was where he finally found direction under the wings of ranting fanatics.

Cambello found ways to rescue campaigns. He helped everyone when he knew it would lead to bigger financial gains. The leader fell into the spell.

Some say his political style was shaped in a Chicago church or oceans away as a child growing up in a far off country. It was said that a reverend honed his ideology. However, it was Cambello, who wasn't far from Illinois politics that beefed up the campaign. Julius wanted the honor of shaping America's president, but the godfather had to remain a shadow.

The image was as important as the language from the podium. Cambello stoked a fire by using the media to inflate the aura of a man with answers. The nation's voters kept hearing the voice of change. They swallowed it like mice after cheese. He was like a spirit in the dark speaking words of calm in a nightmare. Citizens flocked into his corner.

Millions of able bodied government workers sided with the president. They were under his spell. The plan was working so well that Cambello had to pinch himself every now and then. The house of cards wasn't that strong.

Cambello told his lieutenants, "The people are getting fed up with high unemployment. Tell your subordinates to lay low. I see a shipwreck coming out of Washington."

Cambello feared power was eating the president up. The leader was running on tired legs. His speeches didn't inspire confidence as they once did. His words were ricocheting instead of being absorbed. His numbers were falling and the people weren't charged up any more.

The godfather let his men know that a boost was needed. If that didn't work he would dump him.

"We did well. If his people don't fix this image, the money is going to stop flowing. His supporters might even turn on him and I can't stop them. We'll try to pump him up one more time."

A call to the big networks was needed to bolster the news. Cambello told his media people to keep printing good news. Even they displayed a lackluster attitude.

"We have to combat this Tea Party thing. They're in the news all the time. That's hurting the president. We have to deride their campaign. Time to get nasty, you call them every name in the book, whitey, tea bags and old hacks. Do whatever it takes."

A tension was growing between the two sides. Right-wing conservatives stood off to the side in silence watching America trade in values for contemporary thinking.

City dwellers with a high degree of bitches and sons of bitches came to the president's aid. This didn't offset the negative. A political sore was festering in America.

The Tea Party people were gearing up to fight back. The divide between the president's nucleus and country conservatives was mounting.

Outside of the country European leaders weren't in America's corner like the godfather figured. They only wanted America's money.

The movers and shakers saw weakness where none existed before. Some nefarious political leaders poked fun at the Tea Party movement which only inflamed the situation. Democratic congressional leaders were desperate.

Losing faithful seats in Virginia, New Jersey, and even Massachusetts signaled a collapse was coming. Was this the president's fault? The godfather wondered.

"The office went to his head. He's acting like a god damn dictator."

The godfather watched it all shrink like a melting candle. The country was on a downward course, being torched by bad government policy.

He spoke with his banking lieutenant, Lou Gideon.

"This wasn't that bad when we started, Lou. We're in the middle of a bad recession and maybe a double dipper," said the godfather.

Lou says, "Buy precious metals. Gold is the safe haven."

Both men agreed a big concern was in Europe. If those governments start falling, it is likely coming to America.

Cambello says, "My upside is land ownership and private enterprise. I have amassed a fortune and the syndicate's pile has multiplied. If the economy continues to slide down hill, they will battle in the streets.

"We'll still have bars and illegal gambling. Liquor sales would surely rise. This turmoil will signal the Second Civil War."

The godfather amused that many of his ideas were formulated in Chicago.

"Lou, all I had to do is transfer the ideas to Washington DC. They do as I say."

Lou says, "They don't know how to spend. Politicians want one thing, that's to stay in office. Most of them would sell their mother to the highest bidder."

The godfather says, "Their spreading wealth of the next generation. We're catching some of it. They know it. The trouble is the Tea Party knows it too."

Spreading the wealth meant the nation would dole out cash over and over. The government couldn't keep tabs on all the spending. It was economic pandemonium. Like a wind it turned into a tornado sucking the livelihood out of small businesses. The velocity of change went too far. Many small businesses reduced staff, but still they couldn't cope. For many the American dream was slipping away, washing away, going down the river without a paddle.

Handouts for a portion of the population had to be made to prevent anarchy. The godfather knew the stimulus money was being used to prevent chaos. Men and women were losing jobs by the millions. With the trouble mounting the economic hardships would have to be carried by the upper middle class, first, but it had to trickle down to the middle class, and it would go lower.

A few months went by and Cambello called the presidential advisor. He had bad news to tell.

"The president's Waterloo is coming. If he prescribes new taxes, you guys are going to suffer dearly. He's not immune. The Tea Party is now too strong. If the president starts bending his promises, he finished. His people will turn on him"

All the suffering was done in the name of spreading the wealth. The president was almost out of bullets. Capturing Bin Laden or some major event was needed to save his legacy. A major terrorist attack might work.

Cambello was in the right markets. Banks, bars, booze, guns, and gambling were feeding every part of his syndicate. The more bad news was all the better. He only hoped that big O could keep shaking the money tree. Big O was an ocean of spending.

Democrats and Republicans lashed out at each other. Neither party was ready for the sustained downturn. Blaming each other was the name of the game, but the finger pointing was losing support as the regime had been in power for a substantial time. The blame game wasn't going to work any longer.

Cambello didn't know if his luck would stay green. Foreign affairs had him worried. Terrorists might attack without notice even though he had connections. Americans inside the Tea Party movement were having success.

Small demonstrations turned into shouting events. The left had a variety of groups to use to fight back. Unions, government workers, some illegal aliens, and blacks found time to gather. It was only natural that Hispanic and black leaders showed up whenever the national spotlight was bright enough and the TV cameras were rolling.

An army of voices was taking to the streets. The Tea Party's voice was sounding like a cannon blast. The ball of voices was landing and forcing America's politicians to take cover. The Tea Party movement was infectious. It germinated almost on its own.

The country was turning a corner. She wasn't sitting back. The right-wing voters weren't going to take it any longer. Small business owners weren't going to take it any more. Small towns and villages funneled citizens to rallies. A battle cry was sounding on the streets of America.

Chapter 14

FIGHTING BACK

Palmino Franco's business was an example of American ingenuity. His philosophy was an overriding commitment to see the job through. He was going to direct the operation to overcome government's regulations and corruption. The people of Northeast Ohio had to see a private enterprise start from scratch and make it.

Ohio and the surrounding states weren't immune from the industrial downturn. Every citizen living in Northeast Ohio saw the country take a turn. They wanted work and Franco was hiring part time employees.

Richard Stern found a good stable job with Franco. Early on Stern went through many hats. As an independent photographer and magazine writer Richard Stern took frequent trips around Northeast Ohio. He rode from town to town gathering material for his next magazine article. As a ghost writer he would visit schools and gather news of some up and coming talent.

He wrote a few books about his exploits, but hid the facts. The novels only covered some of the story.

Much of what he did was a smoke screen covering his get-a-way. He did not want to completely distance himself from the hazards of hunting down criminals and terrorists nor did he want to be known as a bounty hunter. Giving up the trade for good was unthinkable. Hiding the secret did require disguises. A great cover was being a high school umpire and referee. It was the perfect role for a man with a checkered past.

Few people in the area knew he was an amateur bounty hunter. It wasn't something a high school referee and umpire would broadcast. Bounty hunting was mostly behind him, so was hunting terrorists since it was a trade that he acquired almost by accident.

He told Lisa, a hair stylist, he was a writer. He gave her a signed book and said it would bring her good luck. She said history was her favorite subject in college.

"Lisa, you don't want to walk in my shoes." said Stern, "It isn't easy being me."

Being prophetic, he mentioned the time is right for watching history being made. He didn't say he was profiling and tracking a terrorist that he saw at a Tea Party rally. The guy was in Cincinnati, but Stern recently saw him again at a Cleveland rally.

Stern wanted to get out or postpone the bounty hunting. It was time to slow down. However, bad people just kept coming into play.

At a Lake County rally he spotted a couple of people that didn't fit. The big event attracted a host of people, some good and some bad. He snapped a picture of them with his cell phone camera which he saved to view later. The men sort of vanished in the crowd. Stern didn't know they were Cambello's lieutenants. After getting home he transferred the picture to his computer and printed the picture for his file.

Stern looked at the cell phone and marked a spot on the phone for speed dial with whiteout. It was an old connection to the FBI. He wondered if Monica still had the same phone number, although he swore he would never call the number.

The bounty payoff required he collect news on definite suspects. Stern didn't consider low level criminals as being worth his time. Some deviants were arsonists or worse and some criminals were homegrown terrorists. The latter group, they were the devils of the lot. Stern got into plenty of trouble trying to shadow these outlaws. After the FBI found out Stern was bounty hunting, they put a stop to it. The told him to end that type of work. It was too dangerous. Stern pretty much agreed, but not totally.

The hometown folk of Fairport Harbor knew he was a writer and a person who operated many small businesses. While most of the operations were insignificant, they provided a nice cover.

He was approaching retirement age, so it didn't really matter if people started to find out that he worked for the FBI as an informer. As far as Stern was concerned, it was just another part time job. He was only supplying details about criminals.

Profiling was the miracle idea. The popularity of profiling wasn't too high, but Stern knew that hatching an identity of a terrorist was golden information. The FBI was looking for hints that could provide an early warning.

Profiling the enemy was a specialized profession. Legally, for homeland security forces it was considered against the rules, but for an informer, it was a tactic.

Over a year had gone by since Stern joined with Franco. He added the Sports Park job to his list of occupations. Working for the Oregon Casino owner he watched the building of Sports Park No. 1. It was a high class facility.

As Stern watched it being built, he had some time on his hands.

Stern drove around Lake County almost every day. He saw the signs of the times. In every village and city businesses were shuttered. From Fairport Harbor to Wickliffe, Ohio the government recovery plan was stuck in the mud. It was the same in Grand River Mentor, and Madison. Across the state no matter where the signs of economic turmoil were visible. Closed stores, houses for sale, and vacant land up for sale, it wasn't that way just a few years ago.

This was a picture of a sick country, business sick and leaderless. Share the wealth meant ruin for many small businesses. In Stern's view the nation's president was more concerned about bailing out banks, unions, and government jobs. He may have had a soft spot in his heart for the downtrodden, but saving industries and their jobs should have been his biggest concern. The overall health of the private sector seemed to be off the radar screen.

Eventually Stern returned to Fairport Harbor. Driving down High Street he passed by the old watering holes, the bowling alley, Honey Hole Club, and Fritz's Restaurant.

He turned down Third Street passing Fairport Harding High School. It had a football stadium that was dug out many years ago by men with horses. Their wagons carried the dirt away. This thought carried a message. The good old days of back breaking jobs, yard work, strawberry picking and clothes hanging on the line outside, were mostly gone. The computer was doing the thinking, adding and subtracting, banking on the fly. Mechanical machines, electronic devices, and innovations retired many workers. Routine chores that a mother did were taken for granted. While mom raised a family, most men worked.

The government got too greedy. They wanted everyone to work. The family needed more money, so mom was removed from the kitchen. Stern's mind was wandering. He was blaming government for some of the ills in society. The family structure was falling apart for many Americans.

Churches used to be the cornerstone for families. Religion was taking a beating because of the government. God was taken out of the schools. No prayer, no crosses in public places, Stern questioned himself in silent and reflected on world events. When will the people return to God?

The craziest people seemed to be from the Middle East. Arabs and Muslims were blowing up each other. Terrorists were attacking Christian nations. Piracy was returning to the high seas. Movie actors and actresses, priest, ministers, politicians, and sports figures had reduced their standards. It was no wonder the country's morals were under assault.

Homegrown terrorists were spring up. They didn't see hope in a society that was changing for the worst.

Stern believed socialistic thinking was creeping into the schools. The American system, capitalism, was twisted by the president, his czars, zealots, and professors that wanted change, a free lunch, free healthcare, and free education as long as somebody else was paying the bill. Everybody needed some type of license except the people invading the country. America's leaders were trampling on the Constitution.

Stern's stomach started to sour. As he looked back, calm took over. The more he thought about the past he realized he was blessed for the education he received. At the Catholic school St. Anthony's he got bopped a few times and Fairport Harding High teachers weren't afraid to right the wrong. Something happened. The modern education system had changed.

As Stern drove down East Street, he watched a Cadillac turn in front of him. Another car, the same model and color followed the first. Each car had four men inside. They were heading down Fairport Nursery

Road toward the Sports Park. Stern continued down East Street. A profile popped into his head as if he had seen someone he knew. He saw a man wearing a turban. The vision turned a tiny bit unsettling. Mobsters and terrorists, he thought.

Continuing down the road he reverted back to daydreaming about the government. He was in a semi-conscious state as another Cadillac drove by with four more occupants.

The timing was uncanny as he was thinking about government corruption. The politicians didn't have to inform the citizens that a new enemy was silently creeping into society. They were turning out to be the enemy. They were bending the Constitution by using one party rule. The Republicans couldn't do much, although they weren't without sin on their hands. They spent wildly too. Their war budget put a strain on America.

The thoughts coming out of Stern's mind washed back and forth. From the Cadillac cars to politics and booze, a hallucinogenic effect played tricks with his mind. It was happening again. His sixth sense was alerted.

The high school baseball players were playing a game across the street. He could see Mr. Hites, the varsity manager, on the field talking to the two umpires. He recognized them as veteran umpires, Bill Quigney and Ted Galuschik.

Stern applied the brakes to see if there was a heated discussion going on. Coaches Mike and Tony were off to the side. The Skippers had the bases loaded. Nothing seemed unusual as he thought about the three white Cadillacs.

Doubt entered his mind as he turned into the Quartz Scientific Company's driveway. The cars that passed by made Stern suspicious. Wariness was his hallmark for finding trouble. It was a bit unusual to see a parade of expensive, shiny Cadillacs roll into town at the same time. He turned around heading back to the road where they turned.

Stern still had the government on his mind. He wanted the voters to take back the country. No longer was he deliberating in silence.

Stern barks, "The people got fooled by a two-faced charlatan."

He though it hard to believe the voters were duped. Piling onto one party was a big mistake and then pick a president that lies with a straight face. It's time to take charge. The nation needs a blend of political ideas to govern. The Tea Party has it right. Voters elected far too many Democrats.

As he drove down Fairport Nursery Road, he saw the cars off the highway. They were at the Sports Park front parking lot. Well dressed men, they formed a circle as if discussing the facility. A black turban worn by one of the men stood out as he drove by the Sports Park.

Stern tried to eye-ball everyone. He watched and slowed his car a bit. A wave of uneasiness was swamping him as he spied one of the men. The portly guy, he saw him before. Stern continued down the road. He didn't want to attract their attention.

He remembered his days in San Diego. It was nearly the same setting. An oval shaped huddle of well dressed men acted just like these guys. At that time they were setting up to buy drugs. Back then the southern border wasn't patrolled much.

Also back then the country was big enough to handle the influx of people, legal or otherwise. If they came to America by legal means, Stern reckoned, we wouldn't have as many immigration problems as we do. Now, the southern border has become a landslide.

Stern professed an answer at the time. In order to stop the flow, Mexico would have to fix their economy, police their side of the border, and rid their country of a growing business. The drug trade was becoming big business.

Stern vividly remembered pulling off a swindle on men in suits. He got in on the illegal drug trade. That was years ago.

The immigration and drug problems facing America are still growing, especially in California, Arizona, and Texas. Stern had an early look at the problems as a young man fresh out of the navy.

Richard's flashback lasted a couple minutes. He drove to Bacon Road and turned around to make another pass. As he slowed down, he looked at the people. Some were gone. One man stood out, the big guy. He was lighting a cigar. That's when it hit Stern.

He was the guy that told him he would send flowers to Monica. It was still kind of foggy. Stern was very drunk that evening, but he remembered talking to the guy in the tavern restroom.

Déjà vu, he thought. Stern was more than profiling and he knew it. Awhile back, the big guy was at the tavern for some reason.

"Holy mackerel," Stern whispered, "he's back again."

There wasn't anything going on at the Sports Park. Stern had a sensation that something sinister was involved.

Two of the Cadillacs were gone. Stern thought it important to file the moment away. He'd bring it up with Franco or maybe not. Maybe Franco was selling out.

Chapter 15

AMERICA'S PROBLEMS

Franco and Stern discussed sports, the Tea Party movement, and cheap labor. Stern was trying to find out if Mr. Franco was thinking about dumping the Sports Park. The subject of border security became a hot topic.

America's politicians were caving in to businesses and corporations. Companies used the cheap labor coming across the southern border to pad their bottom line. Lobbying was intense to allow the flow of cheap labor into the country.

Franco says, "Thousands of hotels in the United States need cheap labor. You'll see when I open the hotel. I'll end up hiring some illegal workers. Some will have papers, probably forged documents. Hey, they're everywhere."

Stern was generally relieved to here Franco was opening the hotel. They traded talk about illegal aliens and political amnesty.

Franco and Stern agreed on a few points. They said some politicians decided the illegal aliens (non-citizens) had enough worthy benefits to shuffle their feet on the issue of closing the border. It was Stern's contention that illegal aliens would someday become trusty voters at some point. Their immigration status will likely be justified under an amnesty bill.

Franco said his Oregon hotel had plenty of migrant workers helping to lower the cost of business. This was another factor considered reasonable to him. These were low wage jobs in the laundry, housekeeping, and yard maintenance. The people were good workers.

Franco said, "The immigration issue is stagnating over the cost of enforcement, deportation, and cheap labor. The open areas of the border like in San Diego remained a green card issue. We need the low wage workers, but they have to stop the illegal flow."

Stern said amnesty only caters to the lawless. It was a heated topic.

"They're jumping the fence, Palmino. Is this the way into America?"

Palmino admitted that a bigger security force was needed.

Palmino says, "We don't need the drug runners, terrorists, or criminals. The government needs to police the border. Put the National Guard on the border, that'll stop ninety per cent of the traffic."

Border intrusions inflamed many Americans, especially the citizens along the border and the Tea Party folks. Arizona's governor was taking a stand. She was trying to do something about it. Most Arizona citizens were calling for action.

The trouble was Uncle Sam's poor federal enforcement. It was a state versus federal government sovereignty issue. The president acted like Arizona was enacting illegal laws. The president was really looking for votes.

The Tea Party citizens were asking questions about the president's motive. 'Who is seated in the nation's Capitol.' Neither party, Democrats or Republicans were in any hurry to halt the flow of illegal aliens.

Stern got the conversation back on track and finally asked, "Is the Sports Park for sale?"

Franco said, "No, it's not for sale."

Stern says, "I saw some well-dress men stopped at the front parking area. It looked like they were big shots, well-dressed men. That's why I'm asking. The men were driving Cadillacs."

Franco cut him off.

"Richard Stern, you don't know Palmino Franco. I'm in this for the long haul. I've been advertising. Maybe they wanted to see the size of the facility."

Franco didn't want to bring up the mafia. Maybe it was nothing more than people looking at the facility. Without a doubt the concern about Cambello was in the back of his mind.

Stern never mentioned the fact that he met one of the men. Trouble was brewing. If the godfather's men were in town, it was a bad sign. Their discussion ended for the time being as if both men want to forget about well-dressed men.

Chapter 16

SOUTH CHICAGO AND STIMULUS

The Chicago political machine had worked its way deep into Washington DC. It took a sea of money to wash away the face of the Republican Party. The party was still breathing, but it was a toothless tiger.

Something was reeking in Washington DC. It was the healthcare bill. It was stinking up the halls of Congress. House and Senate Democrats learned their lessons well. They skunked the Republican Party on the healthcare bill.

The godfather had his arms up to the elbows in the political sewer. He was all for government healthcare insurance. The goodness of the bill was paraded around the country. The message passed over and over. It would bring relief to all Americans. The line left out of the statement was 'higher taxes are coming.'

Mostly harkened by his media were false promises. This was done by design. Some tall stories were written about social bills to aid the less fortunate. It looked good on the surface. Inside was the small print declaring who will pay for the program.

The political schemes that crisscrossed the aisles of congress were appalling. It was because the godfather saw the handwriting on the wall. The advice was simple. Take all you can while the shepherd is away.

The Tea Party didn't take deceit lying down. They organized big events by setting up rallies in city after city. The movement was becoming magnetic, attracting national radio hosts. Ideas solidified with TV talk show hosts making special appearances. A concert atmosphere made the events a family affair. Bands and right-leaning politicians came to talk.

The movement was garnering the independent voters. Polls indicated that the message was producing results. Liberty and freedom wasn't to be drowned out by the hard left-wing. The country wasn't so far divided to take up arms, at least not yet.

The president still wasn't doing much to reduce the division. Blacks and whites, Hispanics and blacks, right and left, were moving away from each other. It was a far cry from the campaign speech he used to get elected.

Even the godfather was developing a negative view of the president.

Barking over the phone to a senator, Julius complained, "Don't get me wrong, we've made a killing so far, but he's lost his magic. Don't let him endorse anyone. I'm wasting a bundle on political friends. When this guy shows up, well, you know, I mean when he backs a candidate for election, its good bye Charlie.

"I'm going to be shifting my attention to Ohio. Don't worry, you're not up for election. I'll be sending you a gift. Have a good one."

The godfather hung up the phone. He sat behind his oak desk playing with stacks of gold coins. The political favors had a price. His political friends had no problem accepting gold coins.

Payoffs, bailouts, corruption, it was spreading across the nation. He worked out some of the deals by phone or sent his attorneys to get the wording right. Most of the time it had to be done behind closed doors.

First and foremost government programs were set up to spread the wealth to the godfather's banks. The irony of the legal transfers was two-fold. It killed jobs which helped his bar business and forced the government to borrow more money which helped his banks. It was almost a blank check. The treasury was being emptied by a sneaky, conniving group.

It was thought that terrorism was the nation's sneaky enemy. It wasn't. A conspiracy was being enhanced by the conniving godfather. At the same time he was dealing with radical Muslims. Money was his god. It was radical Islamists and the gullible doing business with the devil.

The godfather's syndicate acted as a liaison for arms shipments and financial advisor for congress' spending bills. Lawyers and lieutenants who worked for Cambello's operation had a code of conduct. The first group was paid well and the others were paid well to keep silent.

His people could meet in the warehouse which was known as the Devil's Pit. Money-making ideas were hatched in the Devil's Pit. It was filling as fast as the golden goose could lay her eggs.

The Chicago godfather had no problem with the idea of spreading the wealth. In fact he was in favor of the concept. He was a poor man once so it was ok to rely on the government's handouts. All the free money would be out on the street. It would mean his businesses would be scooping up the riches. After all, gambling and sports betting was done by nearly everyone, rich or poor. Eventually, the money would filter back to him.

The job for the godfather was to keep everyone in line, even the politicians. He was running the syndicate like a Swiss watch. The cozy network crossed state lines. Illegal gambling houses, poker parlors, and sports bars brought in the hard cash. With millions of people out of work gambling and drinking was becoming a bigger American pastime.

The godfather began to think he could be or end up the richest man in the world. He was well on his way. His next love affair would be with casinos and state lottery machines. They were nice businesses to acquire. He wasn't one to duck away from new prospects.

Even though banking was his forte, he favored sport's betting because it was the underground business that got him started years ago. Small town card games bloomed. The stepping stones turned from mini-gambling establishment to building the syndicate. His bookies took control of bars and race tracks and crossed state lines funneling the profits back to Chicago.

After amassing a gambling empire banking was his next frontier. He didn't totally wash his hands from illegal gambling. Now and then he'd get big time bets from personal friends. The 'fix' had to be used sometimes to influence the outcome of a game.

He'd say, "Every man has a price. It's part of the game. Some people are born to lose."

His syndicate had bookies spread out to take care of the street gambler. Small time games could be rigged depending on the size of the wager. The godfather left it up to the lieutenants to change the outcome of a game. He passed the order.

The godfather said, "Most any game can be rigged to favor us. No one will know if we paid an umpire or referee."

His men were making payoffs from time to time to help ensure the outcome of games. Much depended on the size of the bets. Most of the time the outcome didn't matter, bets were evenly distributed.

Armed with this treachery, Cambello carried the skullduggery to politics and found it even more rewarding.

It didn't take much coaching to advance the concept into the government. Politicians called it stimulus. Paying for a vote was dishonest if caught, otherwise, 'who cares and who will know,' Cambello would say.

It didn't take long for the term 'free money' to be used to describe the political handouts. Politicians didn't call it 'free money,' but they were disciples of the system. They kept increasing programs to spread the wealth. It all fit Cambello's principal.

"Hedging the system by putting money into the hands of people who know nothing about investing is a sure way to empty the treasury," said Cambello to his billionaire friend, George Budapest.

The stimulus wasn't just being passed out to the needy. It was paying bills. Many states were in financial trouble and the stimulus kept them solvent.

The godfather watched which banks were in trouble. He acquired the troubled assets. Then he 'fixed' the portfolio and sold them to European banks. On one occasion he whispered to Mr. Budapest in Paris, France,

Cambello says, "The fools should know these loans are shaky and stimulus programs don't work. It's more like a ponzi scheme. George, keep buying gold. The dollar is going to fall.

"They put so much money into the 'to big to fail' idea. It'll take generations to pay off this taxpayer swindle. All I can do is sweep up the carnage."

The godfather had put the right people in place. They couldn't see the swindle. Government officials were so worried about a domino effect from bank failures they formulated the method to steal from the treasury.

The green light to rip off Uncle Sam was happening everywhere. Tax cheating, bogus welfare claims, healthcare reform, and social security fraud, the shenanigans all played a part in extorting money from the system.

The godfather didn't want the president and his czars to stop, although they were losing momentum. The Tea Party had everything to do with slowing down the leaders.

While in New Jersey, Cambello was talking about the president and his campaign boosting appearances.

He says, "Maybe the president get a second wind. Let him speak his mind."

It was almost a joke. The disbelieving Hackensack, New Jersey advisor wasn't amused, because it didn't help the New Jersey, Democratic governor. He went down in defeat and the new governor started taking action to correct the state's problems.

More hoaxes came from more promises. Change might have been a gift to the poor, but the lavish promises to the down trodden at the expense of the upper middle class was a slap in the face to many hard working Americans.

The gulf between the rich and poor widened. Job losses squeezed the entire middle class. The president and his advisors used a multitude of excuses to wash their hands of the economic downturn. Old reliable, 'the other party did it' was being overused.

The godfather could see America was running up huge deficits knowing she couldn't continue the practice. Forgiving mortgage loans rather than letting the risk takers drown wasn't happening fast enough. Instead of curing the problem politicians kicked the can down the road with gimmicks further infuriating the Tea Party.

Cambello could see he was powerless to stop the Tea Party movement. His people we're starting to fall. Thinking about taking advantage of the president's falling stardom, he thought it might be good 'to bet the other way.'

Cambello told his lawyers, "Let's not stand in the way of our president or his congress. We may have to dump them because they're running out of other people's money to spend."

That wasn't entirely true. Congress still had some stimulus money to pass out, but the Tea Party was applying the brakes, knowing full well they were on the hook for trillions.

Julius Cambello was almost ashamed of the congressional stupidity. Although it was a once in a lifetime feat, the entire world banking industry was involved. It was legal corruption. Politicians, acting like sheep, listened to the fox running the show. Some at the top of the ladder believed their own lies.

The leader announced over and over that change was coming to America. Things will get better. After millions of home foreclosures, bankruptcy claims, and rising jobless numbers, the truth came marching home. Financial ruin, it was coming home to roost. It was here. Change was just a campaign slogan. True deceit was being poured from the pulpit which many Americans drank like wine. The damage was done.

Julius Cambello reinforced the carnage by making calls to the decision makers.

Julius says, "It's a rough patch right now. We'll get through this just fine. The younger generation will start working. You'll see. It might take another year or two maybe three, five or ten. I'm not sure at this point."

The presidential advisor was getting antsy, mostly because the president's poll numbers were falling almost by the day.

Vance says, "The Tea Party is taking on young voters. We can't lose the younger generation."

Julius says, "Vance, what's this worry I hear?"

Many young citizens started to believe they had been fooled. The education money was slipping away. State education administrators were cutting back on student loans.

Banks that once handed out easy money for home and business loans knowing the buyer wasn't credit worthy were tightening up the requirements in a major way. Collateral for a loan meant something again.

The godfather had crafted a giant hoax with two senators to make buying a home simple. The sober reality was coming home. Many people couldn't afford a home.

It wasn't over in Europe. The folly resided internationally. The European governments resisted Cambello's input. When the banks in

Europe started to fall, it snowballed into an avalanche. The godfather said another stimulus for Europe was needed to put the train back on the tracks.

The board members of the Federal Reserve spoke softly. The truth vacillated on notes to each other. A quiet nervousness ruled in the chamber.

Julius didn't flinch when the money woes started surfacing. The easy way to fix the problem was to ask for more money and blame the other guy. Reversing the problem was simple. Raise more revenue.

Cambello gathered a few political friends and dropped the next cure.

He said, "Value added tax is needed. Tell the citizens the VAT tax will put us back on sound footing."

Julius knew. To steal from the taxpayer again was beyond criminal, but he didn't care. He won this game. He already saw the first and second shoe drop. Nobody was paying attention except the Tea Party folks.

They were telling congress to stop the spending. When would they stop? No answer was forthcoming. The Tea Party wouldn't stand for any more Chicago politics or a socialist president. The Tea Party was taking over.

The godfather admitted it was time to move on. The Tea Party movement had gnashing teeth showing. It looked like the organization was in no mood for compromise.

In the words of John Paul Jones, 'They had not yet begun to fight.' The Tea Party members were booting left-wing members of Congress.

Cambello said he didn't have enough money to save many incumbents. A lower stakes games would be better than playing with fools. Congress and the president were no longer welcome gamblers as long as the Tea Party folks were playing.

Cambello's next game was with Mr. Franco.

Chapter 17

AN UPHILL BATTLE

Stern wanted to tell Franco about his real life. They were becoming good friends. Franco was a good boss and he needed to know the real Mr. Stern. He rehearsed his path of mistakes. He wrote down some of the highlights that must be said. After an hour he balled the paper up after reading it and threw it in the trash.

Stern remembered Paula Gavalia telling him personal things. She told Stern much about Monica's ordeal. It read like a story. He was heartbroken as he thought about his misdeeds. His thoughts wondered.

Dogged by trouble all his life, Richard Stern, the middle-aged photographer and writer, discovered a reason to settle down. A son was born from his mischievous encounter. The afternoon drinks and evening interlude just got out of hand. The result couldn't have been more disturbing for the woman, FBI Agent Monica Micovich.

Stern found out plenty from Agent Paula Gavalia, Monica's partner and best friend. She filled in the blanks for Stern.

Monica never told Stern the affair had a nine month blessing. She was too ashamed. She should have been guarding him, not partying with him. The guilt was bad enough, but when the doctor told her she was pregnant, panic and recourse took hold.

The night they made love, she was emotionally bedeviled by the career setback. Monica gave in to her despondency. She dropped her guard and started partying with Stern. The day started off as just keeping an eye on Stern, just a bodyguard assignment. Cleverness and booze combined with perfect timing created the sensual friendship.

After Stern learned that she was sidestepped by the FBI for a career building assignment, his day with Monica turned into a calamity for her. Her partner, Agent Paula Gavalia, was selected over her for the daring mission. Monica was deeply disappointed. The temptation to relax from her duty, to get back at the FBI, to counteract the grievance, was right in her mind. She was going to get even. She opened up to Stern, telling him about the setback.

Stern saw that Agent Micovich was despondent, so he acted like a trusted friend. He was willing to be Monica's listening post. He found the occasion and weakness in the usually tough woman to be in his favor as she explained the unfairness of the FBI oversight. It bordered on a demotion since she was the most experienced agent.

At the time Monica didn't realize that the decision wasn't in the hands of the FBI. The National Security Agency selected the younger agent. Agent Paula Gavalia had the right tools to seduce the Arab men. Although both women were beautiful and shapely, the nod went to the younger agent with the Playboy body.

Secretly Stern was in love with Monica and to prey on her remorse didn't seem fair, but he had his own weakness, alcohol. Once he got started drinking one thing led to another. She wasn't a drinker, but gave in to his offer to have some fun. With the drinks flowing common sense went out the door. The mystic evening advanced to a hotel bar in Wickliffe, Ohio. Monica got carried away by Stern's charm and easy going personality.

Regret took over the next day. Monica made Stern swear he would never tell anyone. It was a promise he would keep for nearly a year.

The sexual act was a drunken mistake. Monica wanted to keep it hushed up, because among other things, Stern was much older than her.

A couple weeks went by when she started to feel a little ill. She started to worry. She couldn't believe her own pregnancy test. Her brain worked overtime to hide the mistake. Shame and guilt built inside of her. Above all, she couldn't and wouldn't tell Stern, so he was clueless.

He would've married her in an instant; because he was in love with her from the very first time they met which was by fate in Buffalo, New York. She was investigating terrorism as an undercover agent.

Stern just happened to be on his own mission as an amateur bounty hunter. They met at a bed and breakfast motel and got to know each other. After a couple days, Stern sensed that she wasn't a librarian that she claimed to be. Stern's knack for profiling made it clear to him; Monica wasn't a librarian. Almost by chance Monica was called into action and saved his life at a truck stop near Syracuse, New York. From that point forward Stern's affection for Monica grew.

The FBI made major gains in combating terrorism from Stern's profiling. The FBI decided to use Stern. Even though they knew he was an alcoholic, but they didn't want to lose 'the asset.' As long as he was going to feed them solid leads, they could overlook his behavioral flaw.

From that point on Stern would have a bodyguard because of threats. The Cleveland FBI was in charge of keeping Stern safe. All was going well until FBI rules were infringed upon. While Monica was guarding Stern, she crossed the line of good judgment. It was two consenting adults, though Stern was trying to achieve the implausible. An older man making out with a beautiful woman was crazy. Stern was quite shocked by it all. The ordeal reached FBI Supervisor Moses.

Stern was called a 'loose cannon' by Supervisor Cliff Moses. He was mad as hell when he found out. He didn't fire Agent Monica. Bigger news was growing. The great shock came when he learned she was pregnant.

As Stern became a fairly reliable FBI informer, he needed protection from the terrorists. Stern racked up some sizable rewards for information he passed to the FBI. That information was helpful in countering a growing threat from foreign enemies. He had an uncanny way of profiling the criminals, sometimes literally stumbling into their camps. Profiling was becoming a favored method of identifying terrorists.

Stern's successes wouldn't be enough to keep him around. When Moses found out Stern was responsible for Agent Micovich's 'pregnancy,' he went through the roof. Stern made it to the top of Moses' shit list. Moses never got over the affair.

For a week Moses was a fire-breathing dragon, but finally came down to earth. The sexual encounter was difficult for the supervisor to handle, because he felt personally responsible. Even though Monica and Agent Paula Gavalia traded turns guarding Stern, it was Monica that made the mistake by getting personally involved. Stern's protection was put on the backburner, but that didn't remove him from the watch list.

Moses still needed the informer. The supervisor couldn't completely isolate the profiler. He had some value, but Moses wasn't about to put Monica in that trap again.

Identifying terrorists was what got Stern elevated to informer with the FBI. Zany behavior, thinking he was an amateur bounty hunter, almost got him killed, but it led to his recruitment with the FBI. He was a valuable tool for the bureau. Cagy and daring, some agents would say. Moses' words to describe Richard Stern were 'numbskull and nincompoop.' However described, he had a knack for getting in and out of danger and finding terrorists enclaves.

He ran with undesirables at an early age. It started when he was transferred to San Diego, while in the military. Drug dealer kind of found him and he started setting them up. Making a little spare money on the side by swindling drug dealers sharpened Stern's ability to cheat the criminal. After he got out of the service, street life honed his wit.

Agent Monica battled with the truth for nine months. Along the way, she even saved Richard Stern's life again, but kept the secret, carrying his baby from him. It was only by accident that the truth was revealed.

Paula Gavalia knew everything. She watched Monica act in desperation, while trying to find a substitute for the real father. Well before she gave birth, a promising stepfather emerged. The relationship with Agent Bill Wright promised to be the perfect match until a cell phone picture of him necking with a young woman ended his charade.

Paula's time on earth was long enough to signal the elusive note of love to her partner. She always confided with Monica. When Monica was troubled by recurring dreams, she told her partner her suspicion.

Paula said, 'Perhaps Stern isn't so unusual.'

He was a man of many trails. An adventurer he was. A man who never stopped to find out the meaning of love and family, he always moved to the next square as if a knight on a chess board.

Paula learned about Stern's alcoholic ways. She spotlighted the possibility that Stern might someday find his way and stop drinking as she had done. Building inside of Paula was a sermon. It only needed the right circumstance to be put forth.

Contrary to damning Richard's wicked ways, it was the encouragement of Paula Gavalia's words that gave him pause. She had a heart to heart talk with Mr. Stern, giving him a level of optimism to ask for forgiveness. She knew he wanted to straighten out his life. A life filled with intrigue.

Chapter 18

NEW ASSIGNMENT

Stern's life as an FBI informer and terrorist profiler was like living the life of a mosquito. It was difficult to extract what's needed without getting squashed. He was sneaking around as an informer. The tense moments were enough to drive a man to drink. It was something he did exceedingly well, although drinking beer and blackberry brandy was getting old and causing him to be a little shaky.

The challenge to be a straight shooter was an uphill battle; one he couldn't manage very well. A new mission was coming his way. No sooner did Stern shake the urge to party with his friends, he was asked to find out who was behind Columbus' decision to only allow casino gambling in four cities. Mr. Franco asked if he would nose around Columbus.

Stern quickly forgot about telling Franco about his past deeds. He was going on another mission.

Franco says, "I hope you can work with Brenda Clark again. I know she messed up, but we need her. She has the inside track on the snakes in Columbus."

In a previous meeting Brenda Clark made it known through gestures and eye contact that she could be a serious friend, even a playmate for Mr. Franco. That idea didn't evaporate from his head.

Stern says, "I can work with her, but she's been in the spotlight and she's too well known. Maybe a new girlfriend will help; someone that doesn't hop in bed with every attorney she meets. I can get close to people without Brenda. She does have an outgoing personality and can really take charge if you know what I mean."

Stern winked at Franco, although he was serious. Brenda and Richard were very close friends at one time. When she cheated, the relationship fizzled. Stern wasn't wishing her on anyone, but it could be Franco's turn, except his girlfriend, Attorney Simone Porter, was keeping an eye on Franco and Brenda Clark.

Changing his mind, Stern added something he'd been hiding from Franco. It seemed like the right time to tell his boss.

Stern says, "I'm a bit of a master at picking out subversive characters. I can usually pick out the bad apple. It's a skill I've developed over the last thirty-something years."

Stern went on to say much about his exploits. He made some serious money from profiling. At first he didn't understand the power.

Richard says, "I've worked on this art a long time. The good guys, G-men, they recruited me. I'm not bragging. The FBI doesn't like to call it what it is, but I'll say it. It's called profiling."

This news was almost too good to be true. Franco could use Stern in security and the FBI. He hoped Stern wasn't exaggerating. Although Franco suspected for some time that the mafia was behind some of his trouble, he didn't want to alarm anyone.

Stern says, "There're people out here that don't want you to be successful, Mr. Franco. They're jealous people."

Stern's mind was going a mile a minute. If he couldn't get along with Brenda, someone else should be his partner. He was thinking of Monica, but he wasn't going to drag her into another mess. He thought it over. He needed a new partner.

"I'll get back to you, Palmino. I'm going home."

Palmino had some facts straight about Stern. He suspected the man had some problems in the past. Franco didn't wait to find out through the grapevine. He wanted facts. If Stern was serious about working with the FBI, he wanted to know about his role.

Franco called the Cleveland branch of the FBI and requested an interview. A day later he spoke quickly with Agent Ron Roman who was getting ready to head to Sandusky to investigate acts of piracy.

When passed along to Agent Bill Wright the story became murky. Agent Wright explained Stern's role with the FBI.

Wright said, "Collecting reward money was Stern's chief reason for being involved with the FBI. We used him, but he was a bit of a basket case."

He filled him with details of Stern's drunken manner. Lost were some of the achievements that were made possible by the informer's information.

Agent Wright was jealous because of Stern and Monica's copulation and the baby born from the affair. Avoiding this part of Stern's past, Wright proceeded to explain the reason Stern had to be protected. Stern exposed potential acts of terrorism which were shutdown by the FBI. All of the intrigue and misery was in the past. Stern was out of the equation. Reward money was paid and his involvement with Agent Ron Roman, Agent Monica Micovich, and Paula Gavalia were history.

Agent Wright says, "Agent Roman and I visited Stern at a mental hospital. He had to be detoxified from alcohol abuse. We hope he can stay off the booze."

Because of Wright's affair with Monica Micovich, the conversation contained some comments that weren't beholden to someone who supplied the FBI with valuable information. Wright's damaged pride, his lost love affair, was the reason he was not being completely fair to Stern.

The subject was distressing for Wright. He concealed his involvement with Agent Micovich, but his dejection over losing Monica hung on him.

Emanating from Agent Wright was jealousy and remorse. He painted a dubious picture of the real Richard Stern. This image didn't reflect well on Stern. Sometimes unflattering, Agent Wright told of his trip out west to the Oregon vacation resort as nothing more than a drunk in the way of an investigation. While it was partially true, Stern did venture on a terrorist camp which was a major break for Homeland Security.

The hospital stays came up in the conversation though Wright didn't go into great detail. After listening to Agent Wright, Franco believed Stern was good enough to be his friend, although he thought he was probably dealing with a schizophrenic.

Agent Wright did provide some incredible information that matched up with Stern's recollection. Call it acute awareness but Franco knew

Stern had a drinking problem. From his experiences in the casino business he understood behavioral problems, whether they were gambling or drinking.

Their conversation ended with a handshake. Agent Wright gave one final warning.

"Mr. Stern has a knack for finding trouble. He looks for it."

Franco decided to stick with Stern as long as he was off the sauce. He called him to let him know he spoke with the FBI people.

Franco says, "If the FBI could use you, you'll be part of our security team. Find the troublemakers, Richard Stern."

With that message Stern when to work. The card catalogue of people that Stern had on file was a long one. He looked at the list of Homeland Security people he talked with over the past ten years.

Thumbing through the list of security people working for Mr. Franco he ran across John Pfefferkorn and Dallas Young, both of whom he knew pretty well. Franco's card dealers, Carla Riboczi or Peggy Lehto, were mixed in with security people. Their business cards were obviously out of place, although he thought they might consider undercover roles as his wife and good friend.

He called Detective Jack Donahue after setting aside a few cards. Jack's name stood out because he met him at the Great Lakes Mall. He might know of an undercover police woman that might want to do some private detective work.

Jack suggested two interns that he had worked with over the summer. They were out of college and becoming federal agents. Nicole Swider and Kayla Jacobson might be the right people, but they were young ladies.

Jack had a sense of humor which he used on Stern. Detective Donahue said with a laugh, "With these two ladies you'd stick out in the crowd, Stern. What I mean is you're a bit older than them. You'd be accused of rocking the cradle. Maybe you better stick with undercover people in your age bracket."

Being a bit pompous and overly boastful, Stern says, "Jack, ladies of all ages like a man of impeccable character. You're talking to an Abe Lincoln type guy. I'm from the old school. Hard work, honesty, and a can do guy. I drank with the spirits of the past. History has been my forte. That's Mr. Stern."

"That's good to hear, old man. Your humility is honorable. Don't get so drunk you trip over your sainthood. Have a good day, Richard."

Stern thanked Jack for the advice. He got over the detective's candor.

After hanging up the phone, Stern recalled a woman he met at the Great Lakes Mall. He had her business card in his wallet. Maybe she would be the perfect undercover partner. She might be willing to help and he sensed an attraction to her.

He called her. In the quick exchange it was decided that her grandchildren were more important. Although he crossed her off the undercover list, Sherry Maruschak was a person he would call upon down the road.

Chapter 19

FBI PROBLEM

For the mafia chieftain, nothing seemed to be going the right way. His party was under assault all over America. His people were having bad experiences with the Cleveland FBI, especially with two female agents. Agents Monica Micovich and Paula Gavalia were snooping around, asking questions about banking operations, and asking union chiefs some pointed questions about campaign donations.

At the time political action groups were receiving stimulus money. A big scandal was caught on video and distributed to TV stations. The FBI was looking at bank disbursements for entertainment. Money was being used for special services, one of which was an escort service, call girl operation.

Cambello's banking operation had dirty fingers. The steering of stimulus money into bogus businesses wasn't a well kept secret.

The FBI agents were causing him nightmares. It was the one group he feared the most. He heard the agents were watching and taking photographs of people in and around the banks. Maybe it was just bad luck, but every time he sent his men to fix the problem, the FBI agents avoided conflict.

The godfather says, "Two FBI bitches are showing up at my banks. It's causing political trouble in Cleveland. And these two agents keep showing up in Chicago. I here my banking cohort in Detroit is letting them look at his books. I'm getting to know these two dames by name."

The lieutenant asks, "What's next, boss?"

He says, "When it goes too far, it's time to take some necessary steps. I'll call Mr. Mahdi. His people will keep us out of this. My experience tells me to stick with fixing the Franco matter. We'll let Madhi's people handle the bitches."

Somewhat in a panic mode Cambello says he'll call Washington and let them know there might be a problem with the bureau.

He says, "The agents have to be moved off the radar screen. One way or another it's going to happen. See where they run. I'm sure they have boyfriends. Get some names so we can have Mr. Mahdi fix the problem."

Cambello didn't take the problem lightly. Trouble was getting close to home. It was taking on a personal nature. Many of the politicians he helped put in office had big mouths. A couple of them were in deep trouble in Cleveland. One was in jail in Detroit.

Chapter 20

CASE TAKES A TURN

One person unaffected by political games was FBI Agent Monica Micovich. She wasn't into politics. Through her investigation Micovich was cracking into some details about Chicago corruption, bribery, and money transfers. This wet her appetite for digging deeper into possible political corruption.

A high class prostitute, a real insider, said gold was being used to pay off some politicians. The hooker had the evidence. The lady of the night was slightly perturbed after getting shafted.

"My man is a liar. He said he'd get me a date with a pro golfer, but it never happened. He did pay me in gold, honey," said the call girl.

She held out a one ounce coin, a South African Krugerrand. She wouldn't let her touch it, but said he was voting on a Wall Street reform bill.

From this information Agent Micovich gathered he was a senator. This made Monica all the more determined. She already had an ax to grind with boyfriends who had trouble telling the truth. They were reducing her interest in finding Mr. Right.

Government sleaziness, lying, and cheating were going on in politics. This was just the right job for her to vent her frustration.

Agent Bill Wright was the first guy to really fool Monica besides Mr. Stern. Her latest miscue was a local man. She didn't find out enough about her new boyfriend, Reese Conway. He worked out at the health club where they met. A smooth talker he was. It seemed at first he wanted a decent relationship, but then trust melted like the snow. It became evident after a few weeks at the club he had worked out with other girls. The fact that he didn't tell her he was continuing to play the field wasn't cool.

Mad as hell after suffering a third let down, she started another crime scourge. The investigation started in Cleveland and carried her to Detroit and Chicago.

More troubling for Monica was the fact that her boss, FBI Supervisor Cliff Moses, was trying to give her relaxed assignment because of the baby. Cliff wanted to keep her out of harms way. He had Agent Gavalia follow up on Monica's work from time to time.

Moses received an anonymous mailed note that said they wanted to get M.M. out of the way. Reviewing Agent Micovich's phone calls and E-mail, Moses found that her investigation was heading for higher ground. Moses added more fire power. He sent Agent Gavalia in to assist her partner.

The case was becoming disturbing for the supervisor. What was supposed to be a routine job was developing into a full blown political corruption case. Some of it tracked to banking fraud, political payoffs, and kickbacks for favors.

At first Moses thought the investigation was good for Monica. The important parts of the case started in Cleveland as a search into contract steering. Some facts arose to parley the case in another direction.

It was off to Detroit. There, banking moguls appeared to have hired entertainment personnel for parties. Tracking the limos was the easy part of the job. The level of the entertainment was sultry on the high side. A call girl service made the investigation more interesting if not bizarre for Monica and Paula.

Monica relayed E-mails to Moses in a candid montage that merely pointed to sorry behavior which added weight to the shenanigans of criminal activity. Even some foreign nationals, Middle Eastern types, appeared to be benefiting from the Detroit bank's extraordinary way of doing business.

Moses didn't sweat the inappropriateness and complexities of the case. After reporting back to Cleveland, even Agent Gavalia commented to Moses in biblical fashion.

"No matter the profession, people will bite the apple in the Garden of Eden, if it means a few hours of pleasure." Moses nodded his head without adding more.

Monica and Paula conversed, compared notes, and join up again as they watched the twists and turns of the case. Agent Gavalia came back again to personally report on the bank's malfeasance. Moses immediately sent Agent Gavalia back to help out on surveillance in order to hook the fish. The prostitution part of the case was deepening. Moses let them pursue the case into the forest, although the dynamics of the case changed. He wasn't aware of a turning point.

The valued customers were moving up the political ladder. An upper echelon sports figure, political jumbos, and the foreigners turned the case from a firecracker to a bombshell. The agents didn't relay this information until Agent Gavalia returned to Cleveland again after two stops. One was in Chicago and one in Detroit.

When Moses found out the salacious facts, he was a little red faced.

He couldn't free Agent Ron Roman or Bill Wright to help. The new hires, Agent Nicole Swider and Agent Kayla Jacobson had plenty of local work to handle. They weren't ready for this level of turpitude.

The case was politically overreaching in scope. The age of the call girls came into play. The young ladies of the night were entertaining well healed dignitaries. If the news hit foreign governments without notifying Washington an embarrassing situation would create a mess.

Moses notified National Security Agency officials and requested their help. At the NSA headquarters command checks created a ground-swell of orders. Political messages passed up the chain of command and foreign affairs officials requested a delay in action. The situation was foaming like a fresh tapped keg of beer.

Moses received orders to standby for instructions. A day passed by without hearing anything. Tension was building.

An anonymous note was pasted on the back door at his residence. It was scary for the fact that it was at his home.

You're close to retirement black cat. M.M. is trouble. Get her out of it.

Moses peeled the note from the glass with his handkerchief and placed it in a containment bag. As he sat at the kitchen table, he let his mind and laptop computer sift through the facts. Now the assignment was becoming complicated.

Moses called the agents and ordered them to stay put and on guard.

Agent Micovich and Paula Gavalia felt the case was still a way off from being completely understood. They were pretty sure news would flow uphill. It was up to Moses to start the ball rolling once all the facts were known. He probably would let the big wheels know that the investigation was taking a political turn. They knew at some point Washington DC officials were going to enter the arena.

Inside of Paula's intuitive mind, she was concerned about the political overtones of the case. This was a big one. She didn't want to say anything too dramatic to Supervisor Moses, especially about her inner fear. They were professionals. Staying calm was critical.

The note and details of the case were giving Moses plenty of consternation. Holding his ground, he sensed danger was escalating to the proverbial hotel's 13th floor.

After finally being notified that NSA was taking control of the case, he breathed a sigh of relief. Their instructions were clear. He should back off the case, pull his people out, and send NSA all the information.

Greatly relieved, he recalled the agents. Moses said news would be forthcoming. Monica and Paula studied the file of the case on their way back to Cleveland. The agents thought a final snapshot was being finalized for a sting.

Agent Micovich was told of a change in assignment. In telling Micovich the news Moses acted calmly. The tension for him was excruciating. He cared for everyone involved, but this one was a hot potato. When he delivered the news to Monica, he tried his best to down play the event. Monica was shocked to hear they were off the case.

Supervisor Moses said, "NSA wants this one. They take over from here."

Monica interjects, "Ah, Cliff, we're into a big case you know. Are you ok with this switch?"

Moses says, "Yep, I'm making the switch. I'm sending you to Detroit. A Cleveland banker said he was fired as Vice President of a Detroit bank after he found the bank's records to be out of order. It's a little bizarre. He claims federal money is being exchanged for gold. Read this file and see if he's telling the truth. First, he's claiming discrimination and second money laundering. With this case you might end up in Chicago. See if it's a cover up."

Monica says, "Well this is a little disappointing."

Cliff says, "Monica, I'm sure we'll know more in do time. NSA is taking control of the case. Leave the entire file on my desk. Make sure it's up to date."

Monica didn't want to detach from her current assignment. She sensed something was opaque. Changing horses was contrary to Supervisor Moses' bible. She could see in his eyes, in his face, he was straining, but she obeyed.

It wasn't all that bad. She missed someone special. She was glad to be back at home with her son. The excitement of the case brought back memories. The greater moment would be when she and her son, Michael, would be together again.

From the beginning Moses gave Monica the leeway to travel if the investigation led elsewhere. He rarely interfered with an on-going investigation. Monica thought it was out of character for him to act this way, but it probably had a lot to do with the political nature of the case.

Michael's father, Mr. Stern, once told her he thought Cliff Moses was a man of incredible insight and integrity. In fact after Stern was admonished by Moses, Stern never tried to bother her again, but circumstances seemed to keep driving them together.

Monica, Michael, and Richard would find out about the insight of Moses. The aging black superior looked after every detective's well-being, especially those under his immediate command and in particular, Agent Micovich. He brought her up through the ranks believing she would take his job someday.

Chapter 21

CASES ARE BLENDING

She took to every case like a beagle chasing a rabbit. That was no different with the new assignment. If the boss wants her to change horses so be it. Unfortunately, she had to travel again. Monica would have to leave Michael with the nanny again. Only two week had passed and she had to leave Fairport Harbor for Cleveland and Detroit.

It almost seemed like she was revisiting the same area of Cleveland and Detroit. She sensed a connection to the previous case.

A visit to the Detroit bank produced good information. Luck may have been on her side. After showing her FBI badge, events fell in place.

While speaking to Agent Micovich, the bank official spouted away like a broken water hose. The VP was new on the job which seemed to support the Cleveland man's story about being fired. His employment with the bank was a lucky break, a reward for marrying the bank president's niece.

The boss, Uncle Sargon, was gone. He was in Washington, D.C. at the moment. After a brief call to Mr. Sargon Mahdi, the ok was given to examine armored car transfers. However, the bank president wouldn't allow personal files to be opened. Voluntarily, he opened a computer file of carrier transfers which seemed to be a normal and routine bank operation.

He gave her permission to look at commodity records, specifically gold. He couldn't see any harm being done in cooperating with an attractive FBI agent. She caught a bid of a break when the new vice president allowed her to examine some bullion records. She uncovered a gold transaction by CAC Corporation (Cambello Armored Carrier Corporation) from the bank to a Chicago bank which linked Mr. Cambello's Chicago bank to gold coins.

The banker says, "I'm running things around here. My uncle was visiting with the UN Secretary General and some people in New York City. He's in Washington now. He has friends at the Nigerian Embassy."

Monica thought that information was interesting. She didn't have to ask many questions as the VP offered his assistance.

The VP says, "If you're looking for armored car transfers, we move millions of dollars by courier. Gold is becoming a popular commodity. I don't think this file will amount to much. My uncle deals in gold all the time. He and his friend in Chicago treasure the value of gold. They're always dealing."

Monica gave him that appreciative smile. She thanked him for helping out. She peppered him with questions about the photos on the walls. They were quite jovial and in agreement on some political issues, although she didn't care about the subject.

In order to keep him talking she inspired the chatter when she asked of his heritage and that of his uncle. She said she was a Slovenian.

The banker says, "Uncle Sargon wants us to be customer friendly, especially when government auditors come by. I know you're FBI, but hey, that's government. He buys hardware from people in Chicago all the time..."

Monica says, "Sargon, that's an interesting name. Is he Middle Eastern?"

The banker says, "It's Syrian. Sargon Mahdi is his full name. Uncle Sargon always talks about the great battles with Israel. Naturally, he favors the Lebanese Hezbollah. He says the war zone is moving."

To Monica the Muslim bank president had a very familiar last name, Mahdi. This and many of the other topics sparked her inquisitive nature. As she checked further, her suspicion started to rise that this case had a homeland security component to it. She was set to roll up her sleeves. The name, Mahdi, was enough to send up a red flag.

Gold bullion was moved to Chicago by way of a private security service.

Further dissecting the transfer, Monica found that dates didn't jive. The commodity was gold bullion. It somehow changed to gold coins. The records didn't match up. Something was out of sync.

Her visit to a branch office of the armored car business in Detroit opened another door. The business was tied to a Nigerian man and CAC Corporation. He worked for the Nigerian government in Washington DC. He was out of the country.

She traveled back to Chicago.

Somewhere along the way the mixed bags of bullion were exchanged to purchase Krugerrands, South African gold coins. It was time to pay a visit to the next link. She wanted to speak with the Chicago banker before calling Supervisor Moses.

The Chicago bank official wouldn't cooperate. After leaving the bank, she called Supervisor Moses. Micovich reported that her case had hooked a snag. With that news he told her to stay with it. If she needed help another agent could meet her.

Monica called Paula for help and she went to Detroit to fish for more information.

Agent Gavalia was crafty. She would change her identity from time to time. Wearing loose fitting clothes, which gave a slight view of her breasts, she fooled the Middle Eastern bank executive into thinking he could date her. He was so aroused; he had to leave the office. During this time Agent Gavalia poured over his private records.

Paula told Monica about her little trick, but didn't tell her partner everything. Although she never went out with the bank executive, her sticky fingers uncovered some interesting information.

It was a day later when Monica got a call from Cliff.

Moses said, "Monica, we have an emergency in Cleveland. Take the next flight out of Chicago O'Hare to Cleveland. See me as soon as you arrive."

She called Mrs. Dragus, her son's nanny, to make sure nothing was wrong. The nanny had everything under control, much to Monica's relief.

Meeting with Moses, Monica was shocked when he removed the agents from the case. A second time, removed from another case, it was highly improbable. It appeared the investigation was going beyond just Chicago banking. Some political figures were involved. Other documents were on Moses' desk.

Moses said, "I can't tell you much. Take a quick look at the National Security documents. Some high brasses are involved in a banking oligarchy."

The documents pointed up the ladder. Moses said that political payoff and possibly corruption was a growing suspicion. Monica protested. She wanted to stay on the case.

"Chief, this is twice you moved me. What the hell is going on?"

"National Security officials are taking over," said Moses.

Moses suspected the syndicate was involved. Even he was starting to worry. If Monica was getting close to high government people, she could be caught up in a conspiracy. It was better to let NSA handle this one.

They looked at each other. The standoff was beyond their control. Moses just shrugged, more relieved than frustrated. He was powerless to do anything more.

That night Monica lay in her bed. She wondered. What's going on?

Agent Micovich didn't take the news lightly. Her suspicion was heading in the right direction. After another day of thinking about the case, she requested a new meeting with Moses.

Moses granted her request after receiving a second phone call from Washington, DC. The conversation was short. The Attorney General's office requested all the files on her cases. They were being reviewed because of national security issues.

When the two met face to face, he was brutally honest in two respects. He told her the National Security Agency was taking control of the case. It was better to allow others to handle the situation. A low profile is needed.

Monica was puzzled. Cliff was either looking out for her or something radically changed.

Moses said, "A case like this is daunting. If the assistant Attorney General's people are calling and Washington is getting involved, it's big. I think this case is turning red hot for political reasons beyond our control. Besides that, I'm the boss. I'm making up a new folder for you. You did well on this case."

"Cliff, I'm on to something big," said Monica.

"Sorry, Monica, it's out of my hands."

Monica resisted.

She says, "This isn't right!"

Supervisor Moses looked at her in a fatherly way. He wasn't normally cross, but this time he was outraged, acting like a tyrant. He snapped.

"We're ending this right now! I'm telling you someone in Washington called! That's all I'll say. NSA is now the lead investigator on the case."

Moses finished by saying, "That will be all Agent Micovich."

Chapter 22
BRENDA CLARK ORDEAL

The disease of corruption wasn't strictly located at the federal level. It had permeated into state governments. Some states and cities offered a safety zone for low wage workers. Illegal immigrants were taking advantage of all the trimmings. California for one was dishing out the good news, but their generosity came with a price tag. They were drowning in debt. Los Angeles and San Francisco were sanctuary cities which didn't help matters. Arizona was going in the opposite direction.

The national issue of immigration was another dividing point separating citizens.

The president wasn't handling national problems very well. Race relations were tumbling. Mexican and black issues loomed in nearly every state. Unemployment among young black men was at an all time high. Most whites resented the growing problem with government spending and healthcare reform. The aging population had issues with medical care insurance and the worry that social security was being wiped out.

Out in the Gulf of Mexico an oil rig blew up. The president mismanaged the affair right from the start. Slow to react in the first place, he turned down offers from outside countries to help with the clean up. Further complicating matters, was the decision to cancel oil rig operations that were offshore. This was just another foolish move costing the government tax revenue from the oil industry and leaving the country even more dependant on foreign oil.

Oil was washing up on the coast in Louisiana, Mississippi, Alabama, and Florida. The government blamed big oil. Letting BP handle the problem was another mistake.

Federal foot dragging was fueling resentment along the gulf coast. A general lack of urgency on the part of the federal government was building between private property owners.

Cambello knew BP slipped the president campaign money. It all appeared to be on the up and up, but the president and his men were cutting questionable deals with BP. Julius Cambello was witnessing Constitutional mistakes. He felt some responsibility for the way the government was germinating.

It was now pretty clear to him that the government was seriously lacking the talent to make good decisions.

The damage was done. He couldn't buy the political people as he once could. Nor could he keep the people in office that he needed. Tea Party movement was on the verge of a Second Civil War. This was his biggest threat. The country's citizens saw enough. They were taking control.

Middle American states, Indiana, Illinois, Ohio, Michigan, and New York had to absorb the down stroke of the recession. Job losses in the auto industry were particularly crushing for Michigan. Detroit started bulldozing entire city blocks. All the way to the Atlantic coast states were crying the blues. New York and New Jersey were paying a high price for their noble if not foolhardy social programs.

All of these money issues had to be resolved down to the local level. Town hall meetings started to plug in the average citizen. Relationships at the lowest level had to be repaired. The damage done by government greed and the desire to be almighty would not sap the spirit of American ingenuity.

In Painesville, Ohio there was an issue on the front burner. Stern went over to Brenda Clark's house to salvage their damaged friendship. If his manliness or horniness was the reason, he didn't get to first base. She explained her reasons for being attracted to young men. Her younger sister was a stunningly vivacious woman, who always found romance. She had an excuse. Brenda was jealous that seemed to be the biggest factor.

Stern listened with baited ears as she recalled the entire episode with Attorney DeLargo. He sat back fixed on her dialogue. She really had no reason to think she wasn't a Victoria secret at one time. She was that type of a woman, perhaps, slightly overweight.

After leaving Brenda's house, he was a little down. His mind flashed back to Brenda Clark's ordeal. Stern thought about a motive. Maybe she was being used by Franco. Maybe she's tied to the mob and is after Franco's money.

Palmino Franco comes to Ohio. He gets Brenda, the Lake County Administrator, to volunteer her services. Then she receives first-hand lessons in political graft.

Stern knew Brenda had a weakness. She did what she could for Franco. She tried to secure casino gambling for Lake County. To bad she was deceived by a two-faced political shyster.

Brenda had the charm, wit, and body to hold a man's attention. She said she used it effectively to sway some committee members into allowing Lake County to be on the casino ballot.

Then Brenda was led to believe the committee would vote in her favor to add Lake County as the fifth zone for legalized gambling.

Stern formed a mental picture in his mind. He had a picture of the attorney at the Painesville casino rally. It was then he put two and two together. Money was probably paid to the young Columbus attorney to make sure committee members voted against Brenda's persuasion.

Stern thought it over. The fix was on. Attorney DeLargo took advantage of Brenda Clark, because of her sexual behavior.

Stern was getting upset. He realized that Brenda had many special skills. He wished he could talk like her. She was a veteran Toastmaster. She could communicate well with ordinary citizens and she wasn't an evil person.

He remembered sitting at the restaurant near the Painesville Park with his head buried in the newspaper. He knew the secretaries seated near him, but they didn't notice him. They were talking about his girlfriend, Mrs. Clark. The office girls obviously knew about Brenda's character. She was well liked. The gossip turned to her weakness for young men. It was slightly naughty. The girls expressed surprise when she started dating an older man, but they knew it wouldn't last.

They were talking about him.

The assistant manager, Philomena Wheeler, made the correct call.

She said, "I think Brenda is envious of her sister and cousins. Bonnie has a new boyfriend. The cousins have good husbands. Hey, Brenda's a great supervisor, but when it comes to judging guys, she bombs."

Stern remembered the girls having a good laugh from time to time. He wished he didn't have to hear the rest.

Patty Mack said, "She wants to be loved. That's her problem."

Taylor Tompkins chipped in, "Yeah, always with the young men, she's a cougar."

That stuck in Stern's mind. 'She's a cougar.' Then he remembered. Mrs. Wheeler spotted him.

Mrs. Wheeler defended the supervisor.

She quieted the ladies, "Don't say that, Taylor. You know how office gossip spreads."

He remembered leaving the restaurant with a chip on his shoulder, because he wasn't a young guy any more. The memory faded away as he drove down East Street.

Stern pulled into his driveway. He felt better after talking with Brenda, relieved that his former girlfriend has just as serious a problem as he does with drinking.

Stern called Brenda and explained some of his problems over the years.

He says, "We can be good partners, Brenda. I want you to be my friend."

Chapter 23

MORE SPEECHES AND DOING NOTHING

Cambello could see it on TV for himself. The president was running on empty. He was losing the support of people across the nation. Dying a slow death was the song and dance about the economy, healthcare, and taxes. The White House garden talk was becoming useless. He was still using tired old campaign speeches. It once sounded great, but the crispness was gone.

The president had hope and change on his mind, but reality struck like lightning. Nothing was changing except the Tea Party folks were amassing an army. Job losses, poor border security, a Gulf of Mexico oil spill, and a bad economy took center stage.

All over the country, Indiana, Michigan, and Ohio, every state needed some new magic to create jobs. After claiming both houses of congress, it appeared the Democrats were wilting. They were still in control, but another disaster was coming.

With each passing day the Tea Party gained more ammunition to remove the dead wood from office. The Speaker of the House came up with a term to explain the situation. The term, 'drain the swamp,' took on a whole new meaning after the Gulf of Mexico oil spill. Canada had loons on the lake and America had goony birds in the White House.

More spending bills, stimulus money to rescue state budgets, were all that the Democrats could muster.

The State of Ohio threw their weight behind a venture that was voted down several times. Casino gambling for the four biggest cities was approved by the voters. State officials had something to build upon, although the idea was far behind other states that already had casino gambling in place.

Brenda Clark's first attempt to lure casino gambling to Lake County, Ohio was well over a year old. The campaign was waged with good intensions. She was the county's 'Lady Luck' charm. Local politicians thought she might help bring a new industry to the area.

Crooked politicians didn't want any part of Mrs. Clark's intrusion, especially because the mafia godfather had business plans of his own. He wanted Franco's Sports Park. This set in motion a new wave of crime.

Franco decided to give it another shot. At the request of Franco, Brenda Clark and Richard volunteered to try again. The same results were in store for the pair. Behind the scene Mr. Cambello and his lieutenants were working to protect his illegal sports betting operation. It was time to crush Franco's people, if not Franco.

The godfather speaks, "We have a very big gambling business to protect."

The godfather handed a box filled with coins to the attorney.

He adds, "Make sure this campaign contribution gets to the right people."

The godfather had to send people to the Columbus State House again to make sure Brenda Clark's new effort fell on deaf ears.

Sure enough, Brenda Clark's efforts quickly turned sour. Unscrupulous politicians and the godfather's lieutenants had their sights set on Brenda Clark and Richard Stern. His men started hanging out to make sure something unfortunate would happen.

For Brenda the personal drive to be successful got in the way of common sense again. In a way the foxy blond caught a lucky break. By going to Columbus again Brenda thought she could still lobby the state casino commission to add Lake County into the fold down the road. She met up with a charming man who appeared to be on her side. She thought her effort was working. She met another man on the casino commission who introduced her to other members.

All the while a hit and run accident was being prepared for Richard and Brenda. A used car was bought, but broke down a short distance from the rendezvous street.

The men on the commission knew about Brenda's zealousness. They were told she likes to have fun, so they were looking for extra persuasion. It would take action not speeches. When one of the men suggested sex, she slapped his face. She wasn't going to be used again. Abruptly, she grabbed Stern. Their fast exit didn't allow the trap to be set.

She told Richard it was time to leave Columbus. Richard agreed. He was profiling and didn't think it was safe to be around a couple of the people. They both departed without knowing how close they were to danger.

Richard says, "A couple of those guys, they were from Chicago. I could tell by their voices.

Brenda agreed. Politics had become a dirty business. Corruption was torturing the soul of America at all levels of government.

The action was no different in Washington D. C. The country was being run by greedy, power hungry profiteers. The focus was on getting reelected not retooling America's industry.

Brenda and Richard decided it was time to join the Tea Party movement. The federal government was out of control as well as Columbus. This was a turning point for the pair. They hoped Franco's business would take off.

Brenda started having fun swaying over her conservative friends to join the Tea Party. Success meant taking back the country. Her style was smooth and articulate. Yes, she was sexy and feeling good about restoring her self-respect and self-esteem.

The Chicago godfather's arm had a long reach. Extending all the way to Cleveland and Columbus, he wanted in on the legal side of Ohio gambling, but he didn't want to lose the illegal operation. His old units, run by Paul the Beaner, were doing well. The small time bookies were turning in a decent profit along the Great Lakes rim from Chicago to Buffalo, New York. The Beaner was the guy managing the operation. As long as things were running smooth, the godfather didn't need to police the business.

Since Ohio's big cities were about to get legal gambling the godfather felt that this would open the door for him. Illegal sports betting didn't generate the money that a legal casino could, so he had his eyes set on a new venture.

"I'll get my hands on one of these businesses. Boys, keep your eyes open for casino jobs in Ohio. We'll get in there one way or another. The table workers will need a good pit boss, someone like Boris or Fishy," the godfather boasts.

He tells his lieutenants that he has a plan to muscle in on Franco's Sport Park, since the woman got away in Columbus.

Cambello says, "The big city money men just might call us to take care of their problem. I got a mole or two on the inside. We don't want to lose out to that asshole, Franco, so let's be ready. The woman, Mrs. Clark, has a big mouth. I'll let you guys work on Brenda Clark."

He finishes by saying, "When you're through, she'll probably end up floating in Lake Erie. You know how accidents can happen, like Chappaquiddick."

His first order of business was to protect the illegal games and his sport's bookies. If legal gambling was going to be allowed in the big Ohio cities, they would need experienced help from decent casinos like those in Reno and Vegas. He ordered the Beaner to find some table workers.

News of a new proposal to allow casino gambling in Northern Ohio sent the godfather to the roof.

He says, "Damn, that woman. This is her fault. She's got a big mouth."

Through his sources he heard a number of towns were involved in a Sports venture. It was being formed in Painesville, Ohio. Franco, who was behind the Sports Park and casino, was trying to work a limited deal with Columbus. Furthermore, it was learned that the woman, Brenda Clark, was lobbying through letters to politicians in Columbus to partner in the Sports Park.

He read E-mails that Mrs. Clark was occasionally accompanied by a friend, Richard Stern. They were part of the original organized effort to bring legal gambling to Lake County, Ohio.

The godfather says, "We keep missing chances to fix this problem."

The godfather knew a Sports Park east of Cleveland was finished. That was old news, but it was the woman that was really making new waves. She was involved in a Tea Party movement to dump the godfather's political apparatus. The godfather issue orders to assemble the right people.

He commanded to his lieutenants, "Let's get this settled. Pay a visit to these troublemakers. Let's stop this before it festers."

Mrs. Clark added Lake County to the Tea Party movement in a big way. She was stunned to see how many people wanted to join the organization. Lake County residents were tired of watching Cleveland get all the big sport's businesses. It was time for Lake County to get some recognition.

The Cities of Mentor, Willoughby, Eastlake, and even Perry had some of the best baseball and fast-pitch softball tournaments in the state. Akron had great women's fast-pitch softball teams. Franco could see the dynamics; he thought Northeast Ohio had the best sports programs in Mid America and he was going to harness that energy.

Brenda and her sister, Bonnie, who always landed the handsome guys, was helping to organize the Tea Party in Lake County. Bonnie had no problem attracting the young good-looking guys and they attracted the girls. Young people were attracted to sports and the Tea Party movement. The entire movement was taking hold. Franco was impressed with the younger generation.

Franco says, "Brenda, this is catching fire. I thought it might fizzle. You've done a good job. I mean Lake County is becoming a Tea Party capital."

Things were going well, too well. Brenda's temptation got the best of her at the Painesville Tea Party rally. After giving an arousing speech, she met a junior lawyer from Toledo who was extremely friendly. She struggled to contain herself.

After the rally concluded, they each left in separate autos with the understanding they would meet at Fritz's Restaurant. She noticed he was driving a conversion van which caused her to envision a previous experience in the back of a van.

He followed her to Fairport Harbor. Inside the old riverside tavern she understood that his father was a wealthy merchant marine captain. He graduated from Ohio State and the conversation continued. After a couple drinks they acted as if they needed a little fresh air. Before long the mood turned to closer encounters. The back parking lot was somewhat secluded with only Water Street and Grand River a stones throw away.

Friendliness turned her on. Kissing her for a time and moving his hand she helped him fondle her breasts. He whispered to her.

"Let's move inside my van."

Like magic words, he grabbed her hand and pulled her. In complete compliance she moved. It wasn't long before she ended up lying down inside the back of his van. The stop light turned green with passion. She was falling apart. She kept saying she shouldn't be doing this as she removed her shoes.

Pulling off each others clothes one by one, they were both on fire. The natural forces moved them to be almost fully engaged. Pulling her down on him, she couldn't stop. After a half hour they rejoined others inside. As the night ended guilt took hold. Brenda wasn't overly upset. Somehow she had to forgive herself.

She didn't dare say anything to Richard, since they were becoming good friends again. She felt lucky in a way. She didn't think anyone knew her at Fritz's Restaurant except for the owner, Iron Mike Stout. The new bar maids, Maureen Wenz and Karen Valentino, didn't know her so they wouldn't say anything.

Julius Cambello had a shadow following Brenda Clark. He called in a report about the provocative speech she gave at the Tea Party. The lieutenant said the charismatic woman found a friend.

He reported, "She took him to the guy's conversion van. They must have been getting it on."

Upon hearing the news, the godfather became nervous and delighted with the news. It was the same weakness that got her in trouble before.

"A dame like this can cause problems. She'll end up poisoning everyone with speeches at these Tea Party rallies. We can't have this," said Cambello.

His Al Capone type personality was pushing him seal her fate. Julius Cambello saw threats to his political base. He didn't like the woman stirring up an army.

"She'll cause a Second Civil War."

Winning was everything to him. Interfering with Cambello's organization was a no-no. He thought that he might use a lover's quarrel to fix the trouble.

It was about a year and a half ago when he had to remove Attorney

DeLargo who got friendly with Brenda Clark. The stool pigeon, DeLargo, pretty much spilled the beans about Brenda Clark. He made the mistake of informing Julius that he was becoming romantically involved with Mrs. Clark. Cambello didn't like hearing that news.

DeLargo said, "Mr. Cambello, she's got a body and knows how to use it. We're becoming good friends if you know what I mean."

Such honest words were poison and a concern. The godfather couldn't afford having a soft heart and loose lips running around. After hearing the attorney's information, he ordered his lieutenants to take care of Mr. DeLargo. He's a problem. DeLargo's luck ran out. He was struck by a hit skip driver.

Chapter 24

START FROM CHICAGO

The godfather always asked the question, 'Did you get my gift'?

The cigar smoking syndicate emperor ran businesses big and small as if he was the Czar of Russia. The portly and pompous Julius Cambello was on the monitor reaching everyone via a video conference call. He wished to add a new favor to his list of political schemes.

Buying special favors was a Chicago routine. Nearly everyone growing up in the Chicago political sphere understood the meaning of favors. In fact political back scratching was epidemic. The Chicago way reached into the highest quarter of national politics. Truth and honesty were disfigured by money.

Sports parks, like tattoo parlors, fitness centers, and health clubs, were growing in size and number across America. It was the newest trend sweeping the nation. Another growing trend was the mating of casino gambling establishments with sports parks. If a state didn't have casino gambling it was seriously out of step. Ohio was a stumble bum among all the Great Lakes states.

Cambello turned his attention to Ohio, especially Northeast Ohio where the Tea Party movement was becoming a growing concern. The bigger reason, he wanted the Sport Park that Franco built.

The godfather missed a golden opportunity to get into the Ohio casino race. For one he was a Chicago outsider and a vicious rumor was circulated. Allegedly, he was connected to nefarious meddling in political elections. He claimed the rumor was onerous. Although it was true, that assumption eliminated his chances of landing a casino license in Ohio. Only honest and distinguished businessmen and corporations could grab the brass ring of legalized casino gambling.

Because of his experience, Palmino Franco jumped at the chance to build a Sports Park in Lake County, Ohio. This angered the godfather. Franco was doing it again, upstaging the godfather. The greed and jealousy was eating at Cambello.

Palmino Franco was usually ahead of the curve. The former Painesville Harvey High School graduate had a backup plan in case the Sports Park and casino didn't pan out. He would at least own some decent property near Lake Erie. Unfortunately, when the housing bubble popped, the property tumbled in value. He was under heavy financial pressure and the downturn got worse.

Building during the horrific down cycle was a gamble. He knew the casino idea was a long shot to begin with. He had another objective. That was building the area into an entertainment capital that included a first class hotel. If he could secure rights to operate an Ohio casino, he was going to expand and build additional ballparks across Ohio. The entire goal was lofty and a long shot, but this was America. He had to keep trying.

Using the free market, investing capital, he had a will to succeed. That was how most Americans rose to the top.

In the way of success was Cambello and corrupt government officials. They weren't helping. Franco was a victim of foul play. Although the godfather stopped Franco's bid for a casino, he wouldn't be undone. Mr. Franco still built the complex.

Through the help of Brenda Clark and Simone Porter, Franco was putting the sport's plans together. Brenda and Palmino were becoming good friends. The handsome man was lighting a fuse in Mrs. Clark. She thought they had a lot in common. Franco remained woefully oblivious to a cat fight brewing between his attorney girlfriend and Brenda Clark.

Initially Franco's operation had some success at the Sports Park. Teams were forming and wanted to play tournament ball. Slow pitch and fast-pitch softball were becoming big. Good size tournament games were forming to play. Franco couldn't handle all the developments.

The last thing he wanted was a rinky-dink organization. Good organization was what he wanted with zero mistakes or bad publicity.

The immediate problem for Franco was to organize a decent set of sports program. He needed experienced help, top people to handle day to day things. Anything else would be a distraction and lessen the chance of success.

He tried to stay focused on the task at hand. That was finding good solid people to handle the big issues. His local staff was good, but they weren't executive types. He had over a dozen paid employees. Part time workers were keeping the building and grounds in order. If he needed to increase the size of the staff, he could bring in experience from the Oregon casino, but that would leave them short handed out there.

Building contractors were still under obligation to test and maintain the installed equipment such as the elevators, air conditioning, and fire systems.

Understanding the inner workings of a Sports Park was one big challenge. He advertized locally for ex-school teachers who knew the ropes as administrators. The selection of a chief executive director to run the show was of primary importance. Franco was careful in his choice. Above all this person had to command respect. The title, Director of Operations, had to oversee all functions of the park and hotel.

Fortunately for Franco, Northeast Ohio had the talent right in town. He found one man of unparalleled respect, an educational dean of administration. This was an easy selection. He chose a veteran disciplinarian, a former principal, a legendary leader, and a top notch academic.

His nickname was 'Mr. Bee.' Maybe it was because of his sting that he earned the title. Regardless, Mr. Franco agreed with William B. Hoover authoritative demeanor. He was hired almost immediately. A quick background check was all he needed. Defiance College was his alma mater. Mr. B didn't let the grass grow under his feet.

Franco just moved off the stage as Mr. Bee handled the job. Hoover picked quality supervisors to run various segments of the park. Managers and sub managers were hired to take care of all aspects of outdoor and indoor sports, field and building utilities, and organize tournament events.

With baseball and softball operations becoming big tournament events, umpires were needed. Butch Lauderback and Fred Heyer were top officials in local umpire associations. They acted independently to take control of umpires for tournament games. Each man had years of experience and were flexible enough to cover each sport. Local umpires were hired by Lauderback and Heyer because the integrity of the games had to be assured.

Next, Mr. Hoover quickly chose two other experienced business managers to work part time on finance and musical content for ceremonial events. On board came Ken Babb and Band Instructor Will Irwin.

The local VFW added a color guard for big occasions and area high school bands played the national anthem for all participant and spectators during opening events under the direction of Mr. Erwin.

Without casino revenue breaking even or revenue neutral was a slow process. Volunteers helped out to make things click. Mr. Babb had family members to help out which proved to be very beneficial. Terry Vale and Steve Babb worked with their crews from time to time to help make things work properly and secure the property. The first season was over. It was a learning experience. It was time to change to winter sports.

Franco's hotel, the Victory and Sports Park No. 1 ran into cash flow problems because of the winter months. Mr. Babb suggested they use more volunteers and find extra revenue streams to stay afloat.

Franco and his associates made the best of a difficult situation. A shortfall was expected, since he was running new Ohio businesses. Summer athletics would continue the next year. He would add outdoor as well as indoor soccer to accompany basketball and volleyball for the winter season. It all seemed to fit, but it wasn't enough to generate a profit.

Chapter 25

A Few Months Later

The godfather was preoccupied by the struggles taking place in Washington DC between Republicans and Democrats. His party was clearly in control, but the Tea Party was ringing some necks. Some Democrats, people he supported, were retiring rather than risk losing an election. The next election was approaching.

Making matters worse was the economy. Although Cambello and George Budapest expected gold to do well in a down market, they didn't expect the United States lawmakers to throw out the Constitution. Chicago politics and tyranny were mixing like a shot and a beer with the same result. The president and his staff were drunk with power.

Arizona was literally under attack from two directions, border incursions and from an economic embargo. Almost unthinkable, the embargo was from other states, from sanctuary cities, and even from some federal agencies. Culpability seemed to rest with the federal government, who seemed to be losing control of the situation and starting a Second Civil War.

'Dithering' was a word used by the former vice president to describe the government's lack of action. Cambello agreed with the VP. The president was dropping the ball on every emergency. The greased pig mentality undermined his ability to grasp the country's dilemmas.

Sitting back in the comfort of his villa, the agitated godfather pondered the question. Where was the fire burning the hottest? He was forsaken by Franco's tenacity and he knew the political fire was everywhere. His White House showman showed little executive experience. A definite omen was building because the president was procrastinating while the Tea Party was increasing their numbers.

Other issues were poking at the godfather's business interests. The political firestorm from the Gulf of Mexico oil spill was a major screw up for the president. Public opinion polls indicated the president was losing support. These were worrisome times for the godfather. The president's lack of leadership was so disgusting the godfather's stomach turned sour. He was biting his finger nails like a nervous child.

The Tea Party movement was working against him. His political edge was eroding. Europe was facing more financial trouble. His Hungarian friend, George Budapest, called to say he was concerned about the financial situation in Greece, Spain, and Hungary.

Reading the political tea leaves, the syndicate's boss was at least at ease knowing he still had controlled over some of the people in power.

Cambello needed something to hang his hat on. A small victory would improve his disposition.

It was time to focus on Ohio and Franco. With his mood so sour he was prepare to inflict some mayhem. He sent his lieutenants to Lake County, Ohio to get another report on the status of Franco's Sports Park.

In spite of his financial trouble Franco used a blend of union and non-union workers to finish additions to the Sports Park. Impressive synthetic grass soccer fields were added because the sport was growing in popularity.

The lieutenants reported back after three days. Cambello's men delivered good and bad news. The Sports Park was complete. Franco's tournaments were starting to mature, but he had financial problems according to the locals. The area churches were helping with volunteers.

The godfather's attitude turned angry. Envy, greed, and jealousy took control. He started to covet Franco's project even more.

Cambello knocks over his stack of gold coin in a ranting display of displeasure. The gold coins tumble off the table. His patience is crumbling. The gold coins don't reduce his displeasure with the situation.

Amplifying his decision, the godfather says, "Europe can wait."

After hearing the news from his lieutenants, he asks.

"Anything else?"

Trying to calm his boss down the Chicago lieutenant tells him some extra news. John Paul Beach believes the value of Franco's Sports Park has gone up.

J. P. Beach says, "He's put big money into the Sports Park. He added soccer fields. I mean premium stuff with artificial grass."

With that news the godfather listened as he envisioned a sign over Franco's Sports Park. 'Sold,' the sign indicated. The Sports Park was now the headline on the godfather's to do list.

Beach adds, "You could buy him out, boss. This would be another venue for gambling, especially if we take control of the park. Just think your grandkids can play there."

The godfather saw an opportunity to not only reduce Franco's hold on Northeast Ohio, but avenge the wrongdoing in Oregon. The godfather started thinking about a plan to take control of Franco's Sports Park. His first thoughts were devious, a power play, maybe by extortion or instigating trouble at the Sports Park. Cripple his financial arm would force him into a selling mood. Some rough stuff could happen to Mr. Franco or one of his staff.

Less violent, but a slower process would be to make an offer to buy a percentage of the operation. It would be a good first tactic. He used it often to take control of banks that were strapped for cash.

He didn't need the Sports Park. The revenge factor, his desire to punish Franco, was driving him. For Julius Cambello this was a rich man's game. Although a small token to absorb, it was Franco's Sports Park.

At his disposal were lieutenants to set Franco up for a fall. Extortion, this was the Chicago way - to stir the pot by intimidation and take him out.

He had to decide which direction to go. He didn't think it would take much persuasion. His henchmen were ready to set up camp and take action for a takeover.

The next day Julius made a call. Sitting in front of a giant monitor, the titan of wealth spoke to a political gallery of relatives and government officials while puffing on a Churchill cigar.

His baritone voice asked a second time, "Did you get my gift?"

The fear of speaking about the gift made the Ohio politicians nervous. Who would speak first? Finally, the quiet broke. A chorus of appreciative 'yes' answers rang out.

Rosie says, "Yes, it's better than stimulus money you so wisely recommended. It's all because of our president. He's going to fix everything."

The godfather cut off Rosie.

"Say no more. As I said, we're on the road to recovery." Julius lies.

His syndicate, the powerful Chicago mafia, had the right connections which ran up and down both Houses of Congress. It was quite a chore keeping abreast of all the political wheeling and dealing.

He was expanding his businesses as the country's businesses remained timid. Constricted by ever changing rules, businesses were opting out, cutting their losses. Bit by bit his people infiltrated into each state. His men set up gold buying exchanges where the economy was in free fall which was almost everywhere.

Julius Cambello says, "I'm planning to acquire a sport's business in Ohio. That's the reason for my call today. It's a Sports Park near Painesville. The owner, you should know him, Palmino Franco.

Joey Ondo says, "I went to school with him. Everybody knows him around here. He's got quite a few volunteers, mostly seniors, helping him."

The godfather says, "OK, I want you with my realtor. Let him speak to Mr. Franco or someone in his office. Let them know somebody is interested in buying the Sports Park. Watch how he sets it up, Joey."

Salvador Cambello, the godfather's cousin, says, "The Sports Park is struggling just like most businesses. Times are tough for everyone. He might sell, but they're trying to keep the Sports Park running."

Joey says, "I'll do it, but he's made some friends. He has a few locals working for him. They ain't your type. A guy by the name of Richard Stern and a woman, Brenda Clark, they're trying to swim with the big fish. She's a department head with the county commissioners."

"Joey, I know, I get reports. She's a troublemaker. I hear Mrs. Clark has been stirring up the Tea Party folks at rallies. I'll bet some tough guys will visit to offer another point of view. We can straighten this situation out."

Salvador says, "Julius, I don't think he's making any money at the Sports Park. You might be buying a pig in a poke."

The godfather says, "Don't be fooled cousin. Franco is trouble. I saw him in action. He cheated me a long time ago. I can't let that bastard get a foothold in Ohio. Guys like him can fester. I'll make him an offer to leave town peacefully. Maybe he'll take the Tea Party assholes with him."

The godfather didn't want Joey and his cousin thinking the small fish couldn't grow. He let the cat out of the bag by reflecting on his past conflict with Franco. The godfather wanted his people to take over the Sports Park without trouble, but he was already scheming with his Chicago thugs.

Julius Cambello says, "Boys and girls, I sent you the gold coins so that you'll remember; this is how we get things done. In Chicago we pay people to move out of the way. Keep your ears open, Joey, my realtor will call you. Nobody tells Franco about me.

"Little fish are starting to grow. So I'm telling you. Franco is bad for business. Every time you hear of Franco, think of him as the enemy. Look at the gold coins, think about getting more money to get rid of this enemy."

Salvador says, "He's quite popular in Painesville and Lake County for that matter."

Upon hearing this Julius tried not to get angry, but he was nervous. His cousin was explaining the goodwill that the new sports facility was bringing to the area.

Julius says, "His popularity won't be a factor down the road."

Chapter 26

A NEW SEASON AND A DEVIL

It was a new year. The small group of volunteers, mostly senior citizens, had taken a couple months off to head south for the winter. They needed a break. Franco would have to use fewer volunteers to keep the park open.

He was still counting on receiving permission to open a satellite casino. He knew he needed additional revenue to support the Sports Park.

He assembled the staff for a big winter business meeting and personally invited some guests from outside of Lake County. Attending and standing at his side were members of his inner circle. His business attorney and girlfriend, Simone Porter, greeted everyone.

She looked at Lake County Administrator Brenda Clark in a demonstrative way, somehow knowing that Mrs. Clark was after her man. Joining the crowd was Commissioner Ray Sines, who surprised the crowd as he entered the hall.

Franco, Mr. Hoover, Mr. Babb and Richard Stern stood next to each other. Seated in the first row of the banquet hall were Aileen Johnson, David Rittenhouse, Tom Hilston, Norman Leskiw, and Jan Urbanski. Although the seniors were an odd lot of volunteers and hired workers, they had the can do, positive attitude. That was the chief reason Franco asked them to attend.

He made one point as he greeted the attendees. Without the senior citizens help he would be in deep financial trouble.

Also introduced were Dallas Young and John Pfefferkorn from security.

Other invited guests were Mark Turchik, David Sarosy, John Romeo, Maureen Reynolds, Donna Schindler, Linda Legg, and Charlotte Cahaney, who came with her dog Truman.

Franco opened the meeting with a comment about the last season and the sport's outlook for the next season.

Franco explained that the Sports Park was a bit of a gamble. Building at a time when the economy was flat seemed like a perfect opportunity, but came with a risk.

"When the new president was elected I expected the economy to turn around, but it was just the opposite, so I'm doing what Brenda Clark and Richard Stern are doing. I joined the Tea Party movement. We're members of the Tea Party of Lake County, Ohio."

Franco says, "We want to take back America. Begging for stimulus money wasn't how the Sports Park got built. America became great through private enterprise. Our success rides on a little luck, but mostly through continued hard work, sacrifice, and the effort from our senior volunteers."

Franco continued with his speech for ten minutes.

"We offered competitive sports for children of all ages. We never asked for government help. It is our intension to continue into the next season of sports."

Franco asked Commissioner Ray Sines to speak a few words.

Commissioner Sines was one of the big gun from the county. He and the other commissioners recognized the importance of youth sports and the attraction of spectators to a facility like the Sports Park. It would blend in with their vision of a constellation of waterfront attractions from Wickliffe to Madison. He felt the lakefront wharfs and Lake County Metro Parks would boom if it wasn't for the economic downturn facing the nation. The commissioners all agreed building the lakefront into the next first class recreation area would make the county a natural magnet for tourists, boaters, fishermen, and youth sports.

Using Franco's Sports Park to start bringing in revenue, new ideas would be forthcoming. A sports center for Northeastern Ohio's young people was a great idea. The lakefront complex was a beautiful attraction for Lake County.

Franco came back again to explain the costs to operate a facility of this size. Casino gambling was a necessary component to keep the park open. He couldn't keep funding the operation beyond two years unless more revenue was found.

Franco had limits. His western operation, the Oregon casino, wasn't a big cash cow. A plan of action was needed to generate decent cash flow to operate the sports facility. Franco asked everyone to send in suggestion for the future.

The meeting ended with refreshments for all.

Another discussion took place after everyone left the banquet hall. This fresh ideas meeting was for brainstorming. It was an inner circle meeting. Franco wanted their input. To keep the park and make it work, it would take money and more volunteers.

Even though they were all disappointed because Lake County didn't receive special permission to open a casino, they had faith in the resourceful entrepreneur, but it was Franco, who was fishing for answers.

It was mentioned that the smaller banquet hall could be used more often as a party center. A large corridor connected it to the hotel and casino. Originally it was supposed to be a secondary casino hall. It had a nostalgic look with nautical and Indian paintings hanging on the walls. It seemed to hold an answer to their frustration because of its sentimental charm.

Stern says, "Let's make it a museum, but not to compete with the Lighthouse Museum or the Finns Museum. It's to complement our town's museums. Fairport Harbor is where tourists should visit. We don't have enough attractions."

Franco says, "Well, that was the reason for building the casino in Lake County. Who wants to go to Cleveland to gamble? This area is much safer and easy to get to. It doesn't make sense to build a casino in Cleveland. People want to be free of congestion. Lake County is the best spot for a casino."

Another idea was to change the appearance of the small casino hall. The building was artistic and eloquent in appearance. It was next to the other buildings that stood half empty. Like the old Fairport Harbor lighthouse seated on the west break wall of Lake Erie, a Lake County art center was proposed.

Another question was asked.

"Couldn't it be fashioned into a land based lighthouse?"

Franco says, "We already have a lighthouse. We don't want to compete with the original landmark."

The land Franco chose to build on once held the mighty Diamond Shamrock Corporation and its neighbor, the Uniroyal Corporation. Building on this land was done many times, first by the Erie Indians, then the Iroquois. So long ago it was. The spirits of the land clung to the property they loved. It was hard to imagine the land once had Indian civilization roaming on it, yet it was the perfect spot for future endeavors.

"Let's build an Indian village on the land."

Everyone was speaking out of turn. Franco slammed the gavel down and called the meeting to order.

"Folks hold on, enough!" Franco said.

Franco declared it was time to assess the situation. First, he called for Benda Clark to speak. Instinctively, he went after Brenda Clark for some odd reason. Even though she went to great lengths to secure the casino committees votes in Columbus and he lambasted her for being so 'blatantly extreme in her manner.' He wanted her to speak her peace.

"Go for it, Brenda," said Franco.

She looked at him with starry eyes, knowing that she wanted him, to love him more than Simone. She captured his eyes. Brenda Clark had a mystic quality. As she spoke Franco was somewhat mesmerized. Briefly, almost star struck, mildly shaking his head, he looked at her eyes as they made contact. For an instant he was magnetized, pulled, almost compelled, but sidetracked by her gaze.

Brenda offered a trail of ideas. She would find a donor in the corporate world. She had made many friends who would surely offer money to help the cause. She knew of anthropologists who might study the Indian cultures in the area.

In the course of the evening Brenda found time to mingle. Richard and Brenda started talking to Miss Porter who despised Mrs. Clark, but tried to get along. She could feel the magnetic field building between Franco and Mrs. Clark. This made her mad.

Simone had to leave for personal reasons. She was relieved that Stern and Clark were involved again.

Simone, naturally possessive, was sure Brenda had romantic intentions with her man. She didn't want to inflate Palmino's ego by mentioning her contempt for Mrs. Clark. Simone was well educated because of Franco's generosity. She had at the very least youth and beauty to outwit Mrs. Clark's ambitions. Above all, she knew him so very well. Simone gave her man a slight hug as she left the meeting.

It wasn't that long ago that Simone's opportunity of a life time, a woman's dream to be married to a multi-millionaire, was presented at his Oregon casino when he asked her out. It got better.

The life dealing cards at Franco's Oregon casino was not good enough for Simone. At Franco's urging, she finished college at the University of Oregon and passed the bar exam after completing her studies in Eugene, Oregon. All was paid for by Franco.

The idea that Mrs. Clark could somehow drive a wedge between Franco and her was a call for action. She thought about doing away with birth control. This was a subject that Franco included on their first few dates. As they became romantically involved, he said marriage was off the table for the near future. If they were to continue, she would be paid well and be his personal secretary and business attorney.

He insisted that she act like a business associate and not as a girlfriend. She didn't create waves, in two words, she obeyed. Deep down she wanted to return to Oregon with her man rather than build a business in Ohio.

The smoldering fire of a cat fight was brewing.

The meeting adjourned with nothing concrete to go on. One idea that did work was selling memberships to the hotel facilities. A second meeting was set for the middle of winter where cross-country skiing was adopted. Some small progress was made at that meeting.

Volunteers worked wonders keeping the Sports Park open for cross-country skiing. Now it was time to contemplate the affairs for next season. This was going to be a make or break time.

Franco had enough money to stick with it. A helping hand was needed. He didn't want charity, handouts, or stimulus money, like some beggar on the street.

Hotel memberships were sold as a way to stay open. The pool, spa, and weight room were used mostly by seniors. This idea bought Franco more time to explore other ideas to generate operating income. The park was safe for the time being. The fight to save Franco's dream was coming.

A surprise visitor with a gift stopped at the next meeting. He wasn't from the government. He had a generous offer to make. The realtor's bid was an eye-popper.

Chapter 27
REALTOR'S OFFER

A dark skinned realtor, an independent agent and confidant, working from Cambello's Cleveland bank, was accompanied by Joey Ondo. He sported a black turban which made him appear to be tall. Conveniently, they stopped at the third Sports Park meeting to offer a bailout.

After introducing himself as Faruok Mahdi, he made his pitch. His opening remark was to buy twenty per cent of the club. Another check would be forthcoming for the rest of the Sports Park.

Faruok Mahdi says, "My client eventually means to buy all of it, lock, stock, and barrel."

Holding up the check for everyone to see was a ploy to get everyone excited.

"Here it is. This is a check for two million dollars, Mr. Franco. My client wants this Sports Park. I'm sure you'll take this generous offer. You won't have to worry anymore. We can continue with a handshake. I know about bad deals. The economy is falling apart. This is a way to bailout from a bad investment."

Everyone was watching. Cambello's realty agent was offering to buy him out. A quiet blanketed the room.

Stern held a hand over his mouth and said to Brenda, "I saw this guy before. A damn Arab wants our park. I can't believe this."

Richard formed a profile in his mind. He felt sure the guy was one of the men he saw driving into Fairport Harbor in a white Cadillac.

The turban gave him away. One of the men at the Sports Park parking lot wore a turban.

With disdain in his heart Franco looked contemptibly at the check.

His response was tart, "No thanks! I don't want a bailout. We're staying. The park isn't for sale."

Joey thought to himself. Oh man, Julius isn't going to like hearing this.

Franco didn't reveal his inner feeling nor did he say anything to anyone about Cambello, but he knew the man was a Cambello tactician, an educated Middle Eastern lieutenant with a bribe.

Some people were miffed by Franco's cold shoulder to the man's generous offer. Two million dollars for a twenty per cent cut in the operation sounded reasonable. Franco didn't even considering the bailout. Whispers floated across the hall that he wasn't taking the first offer.

Franco says, "Tell your boss to forget about it and don't come back here."

His final comment was 'the meeting is over.'

The meeting ended just like that. Franco grabbed Simone's hand and walked out of the hall.

News spread across town like a brush fire.

In South Chicago the news stormed into Cambello's den via Faruok Mahdi's phone call. Neither man would accept being turned down. Mahdi didn't go into details.

Inside the villa something bad was brewing.

The godfather heard the news twice within an hour. Joey called shortly after the realtor and informed him of what took place. Franco's comments didn't rest well with the godfather.

He says, "Franco says, no thanks, no deal."

Cambello wasn't going to play games. He assembled his lieutenants for a meeting. The discussion about Palmino Franco and his associates was centered on intimidation at first. The conversation turned to physical violence. The godfather was in favor of applying big time pressure. He pulled out a semi-automatic pistol from his desk.

Cambello says, "It's time for business, Chicago style. I mean Franco has to go down and his associates, well they have to be punished."

Boris asks, "Is it time for a little Chicago fun?"

The godfather didn't answer Boris. Instead he points the pistol at a dart board.

The godfather states, "Let's start with a warning and finish this by letting them know they're not welcome in Northeast Ohio or anywhere else."

Chapter 28

NEW TENANTS AND GAMES

The steps leading to fiscal trouble were pointed out to Franco by Mr. Babb. Some extra attractions or new games were needed to offset the shortfall. A golf course sounded well and good until Stern said he remembered getting sick by walking his dog in the field by the old Fairport Harbor landfill.

Stern says, "For us it was called the Fairport dump, not a landfill. Could be methane gas is leaching up through the soil. We dumped everything into that old catch all. The rats had a field day eating from the garbage. Here's something else to think about. The Erie Indians might not like people walking on their burial grounds."

Stern wasn't finished. He cracked a joke about the dumping grounds.

"If you put a golf course in there somebody is liable to hit a tee shot off the kitchen sink."

In spite of the cash flow problem Franco saw the wave of the future. Sports parks were starting to spring up all across the country. He at least got things started. Staying with the plan was the only way to succeed. Northeastern Ohio was a fertile valley for sports parks.

Others seeing the benefits of having sports complexes come to the county area were small businesses and the churches. The churches had pitched in with volunteers to aid Mr. Franco. This was the proverbial God send. His enterprise was struggling, but help was on the way.

Mr. Hoover, Mr. Babb and Franco toured the buildings. The

hotel had a long hall way leading to a secondary ballroom which was inspiring. Decorated with beautiful nautical paintings of Lake Erie and American Indians, the hall was a favorite place for spectator to stop between games. It could easily handle two or three hundred guests. Having dances, weddings, and corporate meetings in the ballroom was in the plan.

Facing Fairport-Nursery Road and connected to the ballroom was another building appendage. It would house a half dozen retail spaces. This was an immediate bright spot. Mr. Hoover told Franco he already had people looking to set up shop.

Franco says, "That reminds me, Steve Mikolsky called from his Concord store. He wants to advertise his Redi Go store on a billboard in the ballpark. If he does, the brothers, Woody and Larry Jedlicka from the Fairport Harbor Redi Go store will surely to do the same."

Within an hour Mr. Hoover was on the phone with Mr. Mikolsky and Woody Jedlicka.

The next day Mr. Hoover was negotiating contracts with other parties. Business owners saw the ballpark as a good attraction. One by one, they signed leases for the upcoming summer. They needed to wait a couple months before moving in. The target date was a little earlier than their lease allowed, but Mr. Hoover didn't object. He wanted the new businesses to be ready by the end of May when the new baseball and softball season opens.

Comics and Friends was one business coming on board. Owner John Haines had collected sports cards and comic books dating back over fifty years. The business appealed to Franco because it would entertain the kids and grownups who might want to revisit the past. The days of old comic book friends like Superman, Batman, and Spiderman were fond memories for many adults. Mr. Haines business was expanding. He was already at the mall in Mentor.

A modern clothier, a pizza shop, a sports apparel store, and Jennifer Kasarko's Pencil Box, an art store, was next to a cigar store.

At first look the complex was divided into piece-meal businesses. Franco decided to connect all the buildings, like the Pentagon. Expanding the micro-mall would attract more retail people.

The hotel didn't attract enough vacationers, so it had a hard time standing on its own. Without year around gambling going on money was going to be tight to run the Sports Park and the hotel. He hoped the retail businesses would offset the cost of the building's utility bills.

Hotel guests were mostly players, coaches, and spectators from tournament action. More out of state athletes would have to be lured to play in tournaments. Needed were tourists to fill the void. That would come as the Sports Park and Lake County's attractions gained notoriety.

Heating and cooling the hotel and retail area were nothing more than a drain on capital over the first season, but change was coming. Like the Loch Ness Monster, the large casino building facing Lake Erie was just a legend. It sat empty for want of customers.

Chapter 29

CHARITY BINGO

With the casino issue off the table and a favorable vote for big city casinos, Ohio could start building four gambling centers. Cincinnati, Columbus, Toledo and Cleveland were the winners. There was one big loser and that was Palmino Franco. He did all he could to get the casino issue changed in his favor, but others kept him at bay. The setback was painful since he had considerable money tied up in land and construction expenses.

Franco wasn't one to frown or rollover. As a leader, Franco took the news in stride. Hope was still alive. He continued to have his people lobby in Columbus for a Lake County casino, but it was apparent to him that bigger money people held all the aces. Casino gambling was a monopoly for the big Ohio cities.

The sports complex he built digested one season. The challenge he faced now was to convert the casino complex into some other useful project. Certainly the hotel could be used, but the casino was a building sitting idle next to a banquet hall. It looked like the second unused Perry Nuclear Power Plant cooling tower.

Simone Porter joined with Franco, Brenda Clark, and Richard Stern to discuss another way to go. Simone immediately noticed that Brenda had taken a place opposite Palmino Franco. She gave Brenda a cold stare before settling next to her man.

The brainstorming went on at Rider's Inn for an hour. It wasn't long before an idea popped into Franco's head after Stern remarked about the stimulus money the government was throwing around.

Stern says, "The damn government is loaning million and billions to every poorly run business. If banks and companies like GM and Chrysler can get government money, why can't you, Palmino?"

Franco quickly silenced the thought. His ego or business manner would not allow any tie to the government. He already said he wasn't in favor of handouts.

In deep thought he pondered the idea of a museum using a private grant. As he looked around the room it dawned on him. Rider's Inn represented a way of life. It was part of history. The old tavern and stagecoach stop survived the passing of time. Now it sits in the middle of the Western Reserve as a landmark in Painesville on a well travel highway. It was an old Indian trail U. S. Route 20.

Franco talked for a minute about old Painesville, Ohio. This was Indian country.

The Western Reserve was the northern section of Ohio that stretched from the Pennsylvania border to Sandusky. Going north to south it was seventy-five miles deep. Youngstown and Akron were on the southern borders. At one time the land was owned by the Connecticut Land Company back in 1796.

"This is history. We're seated in the middle of Ohio history."

Porter, Clark, and Stern watched Franco stand. They could almost feel his brain activity. His eyes were shiny, as if a lamp lit in Franco's head.

Franco says, "You're on to something, Stern."

"The government always has to borrow money from the taxpayer. This angers people, Tea Party people and me. We don't need government money to be successful. We have history on our side. I've got an idea that might turn this whole area into a recreational capital like Las Vegas. First, we're going to make the Sports Park a winner.

As Simone and Brenda trotted off to the restroom, Franco whispered something to Stern. The ladies didn't hear or see the secret Franco conveyed. Richard whispered back and made a sign across his lips indicating his lips were sealed.

As the two women walked away, Miss Porter opened up with a salvo.

"You can stop looking at Palmino like you do," said Simone in a heavy voice.

Brenda smiled and says, "He's your guy, I know that. Why would you think I would interfere?"

"Please, Brenda, I'm on to your tactics."

The ladies returned to the meeting understanding their own little secret, a mini-feud was brewing.

Franco, Simone, Brenda and Stern continued discussing the options for the hotel and casino when the phone rang. It was Father Pete from St. Anthony's Church. He said that the area churches were wondering if they could use the smaller casino hall to hold a charity outing. Some church leaders thought the ballroom might be a good place to play a large scale bingo tournament. Maybe they would even use the bigger casino building if the first bingo tournament grew.

Brenda Clark had contacted Father Pete a week earlier with the idea of creating a multi-church sports revival where people from all the churches could unite and play games. Sports tournaments with kids from area churches could play baseball, softball, soccer, volleyball, and other games.

There would be something for everyone. In the evening an adult bingo tournament could be staged. It seemed logical. The Sports Park was ready for play. They didn't need casino gambling, but that might attract a greater crowd.

It rang like a wake up bell. It dawned on Franco. His eyes lit like diamonds as he looked at Simone. She could tell something was up.

Franco held his hand over the mouthpiece of the phone.

"Charity gambling," said Franco to Simone and the others.

There was a cathedral bell sounding at a church. It was most likely near the Painesville Park. In Franco's mind a white dove landed. It brought a sign from heaven like the dove appearing to Noah.

Franco talked fast into the phone, almost rushing, "Thanks, Father Pete, you just gave me an idea. I'll get back to you tomorrow at the latest."

Franco hung up the phone. With a big smile on his face he said, "We're going to have gambling at the small casino."

Simone says, "We're not allowed to gamble. What're you talking about, a small casino?"

Visualizing the ballroom full of guests, tables filled with gamblers, blackjack players, and roulette wheels spinning. Franco turns to Simone with his idea.

He says again, "Charity gambling, Simone. We won't be running the casino or the card games. The churches will. We'll ask the local churches to help fund the Sports Park with bingo revenue and God only knows how big it could grow."

It didn't take long to convert the smaller ballroom into a mini-casino. Tables were set up for bingo. After two days of arranging furnishings, the ballroom was nearly ready for patrons.

News spread that Lake County churches were sponsoring a weekend bingo tournament. The news was rippling across the county. Tickets for opening night sold out then the weekend was sold out. Even the hotel, which was closed on weekdays, was busy on the weekends with reservations being made for out of town guests.

Although most of the participants were senior citizens, it was the start of something big. So successful was the first program that the area churches agreed to another weekend of bingo. The games expanded over the weekend. Blackjack and poker tables were set up in another room to diversify the games offered.

Again the weekend was sold out. Excitement was building week after week. It appeared that Charity Bingo was the miracle Franco needed to keep the park financially solvent. Mr. Babb concurred as he crushed the numbers.

Mr. Babb says, "Palmino, you're Sports Park is almost in the black. I think you're going to make it."

The Sports Park had another month to go before the small businesses would be operating. It was almost a given that baseball and softball tournaments would make the whole operation a profitable venture.

Franco was delighted by the news. The news travelled fast. In Chicago the war drums were beating.

Chapter 30

CAMBELLO'S WARNING

Church gambling at Franco's non-profit gambling hall was helping to keep the Sports Park operating. Bingo expanded to every evening. Church festivals were planned for nearly every weekend.

This didn't sit well with local bookies and the card houses where illegal gambling turned a sizable profit for the godfather's syndicate. One bookie, the Horse, complained to John Paul Beach, alias, the Beaner, and he reported to the godfather that Franco's church gambling was hurting Northeast Ohio's underground card games.

Cambello was concerned, but that wasn't the real reason the godfather wanted Franco's now flourishing business.

Palmino Franco's gambling hall was ahead of the curve. He turned the casino hall over to the churches. The charity casino and hotel was helping to support the Sports Park.

Gambling was coming for Cleveland, but it would take time. The godfather knew this would harm his illegal gambling business. He called a teleconference meeting to explain the predicament for his Ohio operation.

The godfather says, "Folks, I see two problems. Now that Ohio voters have approved casinos for the big Ohio cities my games will be under pressure. Right now, Franco is hurting my card houses. This is small right now, but I don't want it to fester. The local bookies are mad because Franco's gambling hall is stealing customers. I tried to buy him out. The racetracks aren't doing well even though we installed slot machines. When the big casinos open, the card houses will suffer even more."

The godfather explained how he had helped the state politicians win elections. He knew everyone in his party was feeling the political pinch because of high unemployment and the Tea Party movement.

The godfather says, "I'm supplying you with campaign funds to fight the Tea Party movement. You work for me from time to time and more gold coins will come your way. You do want your campaigns financed, don't you?"

Rosie says, "You know we do, Mr. Cambello."

Not wishing to beat around the bush any longer, the godfather states his case.

"Palmino Franco, I say, he's trouble. He's not backing down even when I offered him a fair price. It's too bad he built the casino and Sports Park in Lake County. I'm going to take some action."

Salvador asks, "What are you planning to do?"

The godfather states, "He's liable to turn that operation into a gold mine. I still want to buy him out, but he's trying to pull a fast one with charity gambling. He's got to be shutdown.

"Sal, you're over there in Fairport Harbor. Why don't you ask the mayor to pull the plug on this business? Let him know a reward will come his way if he does."

The request was preposterous. Fairport Harbor wanted to annex some of the property. There were complications involved, environmental issues.

Chicago politics wouldn't work in Lake County let alone the Village of Fairport Harbor. The mayor would never go along with the bribe.

Salvador and the local politicians knew Mr. Franco. Even though Franco failed to get real casino gambling in Lake County, he impressed the locals. His casino setback didn't stop him from switching to a quality non-profit gambling operation.

The churches were operating the low stakes gambling hall. It was where people could play games for little money on any given day. Some senior citizens called it 'a retreat,' others said it was their 'campground.' The local churches took turns running the games. Money was being made from renting the hall which helped to pay for the Sports Park. In addition they were reserving rooms at the hotel for relatives.

Cambello asks, "Are you guys thinking about this problem?"

The godfather waited for an answer to come back. There was a long pause, as if everyone was struck by lightning.

The Columbus attorney, Devlin Culliver, jumps in, "Julius, you're asking for the moon. They're operating within the law. You can't ask the mayor or the Painesville Township trustees to just shut them down. It's non-profit gambling. They're allowed to gamble as a non-profit organization, strictly low stakes."

Rosie says, "It's all legal, they're mostly playing bingo, Mr. Cambello."

That wasn't the right answer. The mafia leader fingered his table as if playing a piano. Trying to be crafty and cool-headed, he says, "You have to do a little better than that, so let's try again. We need to do things my way, the Chicago way."

The Cleveland politician danced around the issue. He knew Lake County had a reputation for doing things on the up and up. The other politicians argued that it was out of their jurisdiction. Parroting excuses one after another, they couldn't agree on a fix.

Nobody was going to stick their neck out. If the godfather wanted things done Chicago style, he would have to go for it alone. Franco's non-profit gambling hall was too popular.

The godfather tried to play the ethnic card. He heard Painesville had a strong base of Mexican card players.

The godfather says, "Maybe the Mexicans will work for me. They might want to stir up some trouble for the right price."

Attorney Bill Whayler finally says, "Don't do it, you're stepping on Christians. They won't go for it."

The godfather asks, "Isn't there a law being violated?"

Whayler says, "Listen, I know a public defender, Dave Farren. Dave's a fair man. I'll ask Dave to talk with the Lake County Commissioners to see if something is wrong with the operation."

"Mr. Cambello, this isn't Chicago. They're straight shooters in Lake County. Don't expect Mr. Farren to come back with a miracle."

Angrily the godfather protests, "Everyone has a price! You find the weak link."

That ended the conference call.

Mr. Whayler followed up with a candid conversation to Attorney

Dave Farren. He shot down any idea of collaborating, corruption, or about any meddling in church affairs. Mr. Farren called Brenda Clark with news of a bribe. She told him the commissioners would never stand for any bribery. They won't mess with the churches or their non-profit games. Bingo and festivals bring in decent money. It was all non-profit games.

Mr. Whayler called the godfather with the news.

"The churches are running moderately low budget fund raisers, festivals, strictly legal games to keep the Sports Park open. The judges, commissioners, and police let their children and grandkids play baseball, softball, and soccer at the Sports Park. The commissioners see nothing wrong. They won't touch this operation."

The godfather explained again. Over and over he said the non-profit gambling was hurting his business. He started to lose his temper.

Speaking from his luxurious estate in South Chicago he said he might have to make a personal visit to Ohio.

The godfather says, "Listen Whayler, I don't know anything about Painesville, Ohio except what my people tell me. I got gambling operations in Northeast Ohio and in other big cities. These guys say the church gambling is hurting business. You guys are making excuses. I say Franco is trouble. Now I'm starting to get a little mad, so let's try something else."

Explaining his idea, the godfather says a visit from his lieutenants might help.

"In Chicago we operate different than you, Whayler. We have to make a point you know. We'll shake some people up. Maybe Franco or one of his people will get the message."

Attorney Whayler says, "Sheriff D won't have it."

The godfather commands, "I get things done, Whayler! It's done my way."

Whayler says, "Hey, you need to cool off!"

The godfather says, "Don't worry, everything will be ok."

Whayler says, "Don't start anything here. The sheriff won't stand for it. They'll be on you like flies on shit."

The godfather makes one last plea. He beckons respect.

He says, "I'll buy the place. You'll see. My donations will keep your park working. I'm going to help the church people, the seniors, and everyone. You'll be rewarded when people see things our way.

Whayler says, "You're mad because he doesn't want to sell."

"I say everybody has a price, do you agree?" The godfather asks.

Mr. Whayler says, "This isn't Chicago, Mr. Cambello. That's the problem."

Frustrated, a steamy voice was taking hold. The godfather answers.

The godfather says angrily, "Oh, yeah! OK, my lieutenants will be coming to Ohio. We have a business to run. I'm not going to have a bunch of bible thumpers messing things up."

The impact from his closing message left Mr. Whayler to wonder if the godfather would follow up with his threat. He didn't think the godfather would be so dumb as to interfere with Franco's business.

The mafia chief ended the meeting and went to work with his men. He was up to his old tricks. He wasn't going to let the dust settle.

He says, "I saw the broad on TV, Brenda Clark. She's a sexy blond, who works for Franco and the Tea Party. We can set something up, an accident, a boyfriend problem, or a person of interest will strengthen our point of view. We have options."

Chapter 31

ANOTHER BID

As the good news spread, Franco had a deep suspicion his rival was closing in. It was Stern who gave him a warning. The fact that Stern might have seen Cambello's people in the area made Franco a little worried. If Cambello was behind the bid or one of his associates, he could make life difficult. Franco didn't want a fight nor was he ready to push the panic button; however, the plot thickened.

A donation came by certified mail to the office in a brown envelope. Miss Porter signed for the packet. Inside the envelope Simone Porter found ten one hundred dollar bills in serial order with a note and address clipped to the bills.

Dear Mr. Franco:

My name is Sargon Mahdi.

Money comes your way. I have the serial numbers of the one hundred dollar bills if you wish to return them. First, let me explain.

I hear people are bidding for your property. If your business is for sale (Sports Park) property, we are prepared to buy it. I'm stepping in front of the line. A fair price is about $7,000.000.00 which should get your attention. With this offer I'd say you are off the hook, but I'm not through.

I have a friend coming to talk with you or your representative. Please let me bid on this complex, since I'm on your side. Julie will be calling a few weeks. We're gathering up the money for a deal. Don't sell until you hear from us.

Sincerely,

Sargon.

P.S. Better yet, I will double the offer if you meet my representative and sign a deal on the spot. She will have the paperwork and a check for you. You must sign and hold the Quick Claim Deed at that time. Give Julie a copy. After the check clears the bank, we'll be the owners.

Simone didn't know what to say. She presented Franco with the cash and note as he entered the office. As he reads the note, she watches his expression.

Simone says, "Are you surprised? This might be a good deal. Let's talk with her."

Franco says, "My guess is - it could be a setup."

Simone pleads, "Palmino, it's a second bid, come on. We can go back to Oregon. I think you should meet Julie."

Franco says, "So they can shoot me in the back."

Simone asks, "What? Why?"

Franco could see the worry on her face as he lowers the note.

The question she wants to ask is driving her crazy. She wonders why he's hiding something from her. She looks at her man trying to figure him out. Her wondering turns to fear as she wants to know.

Simone asks, "What going on, Palmino?"

Franco says, "Maybe this note is just a warning, Simone. You don't know enough about the past, some trouble happened in Oregon long ago, so I'll leave it that way for now. You don't need to concern yourself with water over the dam."

Franco went in another room and called Mr. Stern. He told him the news. They discussed the name Sargon Mahdi and whether the deal was legitimate. After fifteen minutes on the phone Franco returned to Simone's office.

Franco says, "Stern is good at negotiating these types of crazy deals."

Simone cringes and expresses some shock.

"You're going to let Mr. Stern talk for you?" Simone asks.

"I don't trust anyone at this point. I shouldn't be nervous, because the Sports Park isn't for sale, but I'll say this. I'm not a fool. We'll let Mr. Stern talk for us. If they write in the right numbers I'm done with this Sports Park."

Simone cheers, "Yes!"

Franco says, "The way the government is running the country, who would blame me for selling out? They're going to raise taxes on everything.

"Government corruption is making me think this way and the people we're dealing with are probably corrupt too. You don't know how greedy and ruthless people can be."

Simone bemoans the effort building the Sports Park.

She says, "I'm glad you're thinking about selling out? I mean, that's ok. We can go back to Oregon. Don't you want to go back to Oregon?"

He bypasses the question.

Palmino says, "Hopefully, it's not a trick. No funny stuff, this deal is for real. I'll have security on the scene. Dallas Young and Pfefferkorn will be point men on our side. You leave after this woman calls. Go to the mall shopping or something. I'm going to watch this meeting unfold. Stern will be the only talker for us. I'm sure they know we will be monitoring this meeting."

Simone says, "I can't believe Richard Stern is your negotiator."

She asks, "Is he up for this? I think this is out of his league."

Franco says, "Yes, he's up for this! Yes, it's a bit strange."

Franco says, "Simone, he's been through scary battles in his days. Let me tell you something about Mr. Stern. He told me about Jose Lopez, a federal agent, who saved his life in San Diego. Lopez told him to leave San Diego, before he gets shot. Apparently he listened to Agent Lopez. That was long ago.

"I think Stern said he moved to Reno and got married and divorced in the same year. He came back to Ohio. At that point he said a restaurant owner, Jimmy DeAngello, from Macedonia taught him to be a gourmet cook."

Simone asks, "Do you believe all this?"

Franco asks, "Do you want more?"

Simone nods her head as she listens to Franco.

"We're at Fritz's Restaurant in Fairport Harbor. Now the story gets corny. He's talking about a Finnish ghost named Hilston. The bar owner, Mike Stout says the ghosts are in his restaurant. They both say the ghost of Mr. Hilston fooled the terrorists.

"Even Stout says that he knows of more ghost incidents in his restaurant. Stout says Horst Beamer was killed by terrorists. He was a Fairport Harbor administrator, who was supposedly gunned down by terrorists. Somehow Stern was connected to this murder. There is a bunch of mystery surrounding Mr. Stern.

"I'm not sure how the conversation got to Eastlake, Ohio, but Stern said two bar maids, Maureen Wenz and Karen Valentino, waited on the terrorists. Stern wasn't talking straight, because he was drunk. That's when I told him he had to quit drinking or he was out of our organization. That's another story."

Simone says, "Ghosts, please!"

Franco says, "Wait!"

Franco continued with the story about the FBI and Stern.

"I can go on with names of FBI agents that know Mr. Stern. I talked with them in Cleveland. Agent Bill Wright told me that he was an informer.

"Stern said terrorists crossed Lake Erie and landed in Fairport Harbor at the port authority boat ramp. They were plotting an attack on the Perry Nuclear Plant. The FBI broke up the terrorist ring.

"Take a look at what's going on." Franco says.

"Simone, here is the connection. It's the name.

"Stern named off the last name of known terrorists, the Mahdi Brothers. Do you see the connection with the people that are bidding for the property?"

At first Simone reacted with amazement as the name Mahdi came to light. She wasn't entirely on the same page, but wanted to be on the safe side.

She says, "I think you better call the FBI."

"Not yet, Simone, we're going to wait. This could end up being big. Stern is willing to take the chance. He's done this before.

"The FBI told me Stern has a habit of finding trouble. The files he keeps on people are loaded with known terrorists. That's how he can pick out the criminals if that's what you want to call these radicals. Profiling is his trademark. He uses a profile of terrorists to track them down. He'll contact the Cleveland FBI soon and he said he knows a couple of agents that live in Fairport."

Simone wasn't buying the story. She just wanted Palmino to get out before something weird happens. Good deals only come on rare occasions. She saw legal problems, especially the way Stern was identifying people.

Simone says, "I don't like this. Racial profiling, it's against the law. We're most likely just dealing with rich foreigners that have the same name. They're probably not terrorists. These people are probably just filthy rich and want your business."

Franco says, "Well, that may be true, I agree, but if they're terrorists, well, let's not go there. We'll let Stern do the profiling. The FBI will handle this if it isn't legit. Stern says he's done this many times. He might be half crazy, but his track record seems to be on the up and up. Let's have some confidence in his judgment."

Simone says, "I'm leaning on the safe side, yet, I don't know. Don't you think you should call the FBI?"

Franco answers, "No, Simone, Stern wants to get more information and maybe get a reward. I own the Sparks Park. I want to see the numbers these people put up. If there's trouble, Stern is taking the risk, not us."

Chapter 32

SET UP FOR TRAGEDY

"Boris, you, Lou and the boys will remove any doubt about our intentions."

The godfather explains to his toughs that it's time to lay down the law, Chicago style.

"Boys, I mean business. I'm beginning to see a Lake Erie tragedy about to happen. Too bad is all I can say."

The lieutenants sat around the table planning the operation.

The godfather continues, "The casino hall will be closed for good. I'm going to shut this guy down. I've hired a couple men to reduce the size of the Sports Park. After the job is done the Sports Park won't have the revenue to stay open. Somebody will have to sell if Franco isn't around.

"I've hired specialists. I call them specialists for a reason. They know fire alarm systems and how to start a fire. They'll be infiltrated into the complex.

"The specialists will make some night time adjustments to the alarm systems. They're like you, Boris, they're foreigners. My banking friend told me to hire these professionals. He said he's used them to torch buildings. So, I've recruited these guys. Apparently, they don't mess around.

"They come from Detroit. They don't speak much English. I don't know how they got in this country."

The godfather's plan was to burn down the gambling hall. Boris was quite handy at creating fires, but Franco didn't want to use Boris for fear he would mess things up.

Cambello says, "Boris, you come into the plan real quick. I know you're a fire bug, but I have a special mission for you and the boys. Your team is going to take care of Mrs. Clark and her boyfriend. They're going to have a lovers quarrel with an awful outcome."

"Beaner, you meet the specialists in Detroit. Take the fire starters to the Sports Park. Point out the buildings that need to go. If they get caught make sure you're far away from the scene.

"Boris, find Brenda Clark and her boyfriend.

"I've rented a hotel for a month, so you guys can rehearse the jobs."

Cambello wasn't going to let Franco get away. That was a separate job. A professional sniper was hired to remove Franco.

The burly men left the South Chicago villa and headed for the Ohio border in three cars. The godfather's toughs drove nonstop to Mentor. The unpleasantness was about to erupt on Franco, the Sports Park, and his staff. Boris and Lou were in charge of one group. The assassin drove in a separate car.

Beaner drove to Detroit and met the fire starters. The two Iranians rented a car and followed Mr. Beach. Everyone met at a hotel in Mentor, Ohio.

Boris sent a text message to Julius.

We're near the location, setting up the hit.

The godfather wanted to make sure everyone was set.

Calling Boris, he says, "Boris, I have a satellite view of the area. You and Lou drive to Fairport Harbor. You park and watch from East Street. Park down by New Fourth Street and let the boys practice by walking around at night. It's all about timing. Tell the boys to get this right, not like the boner you pulled in Willowick, Ohio."

Boris exclaims, "But boss, I didn't know the bitch was going to sell her house. Maybe she got away, but so did I, right!"

"Don't mess this up, Boris! I want Franco and his people out of the way. We have time to practice. Make sure you collect and delete all the messages on the phones. You have to pull out the batteries and ditch the cell phones. You'll have the only working phone.

"You drive away when the fun begins. Let the boys handle this. If they get caught you and Lou will be long gone."

Boris says, "OK, boss. I'll call after the jobs are done."

Cambello wasn't hurrying for a change. Rushing to get things done was a common mistake for him. Too often it led to operational mistakes.

He had other things on his mind like the growing Tea Party movement. This was adding to his frustration.

The godfather was having second thoughts about the man in the White House. His political problems were cropping up. Because of the Tea Party movement, the godfather didn't think he could save many of his political puppets.

Congress and the president acted as if the economy and unemployment were too big to solve. The stimulus bill provided money for Cambello's union people and the unemployed, but it wasn't going to last forever. The Tea Party saw the borrowing as a sign of weakness.

Although government spending was good for the gold market, it had a negative effect on the party. Some Democrats that he backed kept retiring from office rather than face an election defeat. This was akin to defections in the army.

The Second Civil War was beginning. The Tea Party was placing the administration in a headlock. Cambello and George Budapest knew full well tyranny wasn't going to replace the American spirit. The winds of change were shifting. He knew his people were going to be ousted in the next election.

Spending bills were stalling in committees. His union people were feeling the slow down. Cambello wasn't making money like he once did. Primary elections weren't going his way either. Because of the Tea Party movement his hold on political power was diminishing.

The generals inside the Tea Party were directing the political fight. The battles weren't fought on the streets with live ammunition, yet. They were on the offensive with verbal attacks.

This was going to change. The godfather figured it was time to distract the Tea Party movement. His regular lieutenants were setting up for an Ohio fight. He had mercenaries on his side.

He called Mr. Mahdi. It was time for Mahdi's Islamic friends to start some agitation. This in turn this would increase arms sales and the price of gold would rise on the world market.

The days and weeks pass as the lieutenants wait for final orders.

Chapter 33
TIMING PLAY

Not all was going according to plan. Cambello had to move the assassin on the fly. The timing of the entire operation slipped, but seemed to be working in the godfather's favor; except Franco wasn't alone and didn't travel as expected.

The assassin was waiting for Franco to appear, but he was with Miss Porter and another person. The assassin's aim was blocked; he couldn't take the shot as he had hoped. They would go to the backup plan. He's told to join Beaner.

The godfather orders Beaner to finalize the operation. It was time to send in the specialists. The previous night, while the night watchman was smoking a cigarette behind the guardhouse, they took advantage of the situation. Adjustments were made to the security system that made it possible to operate with impunity.

The godfather says, "Beaner, just make sure these guys burn down the right places. Let all the evidence burn up. I mean all."

The godfather says the assassin is coming to join them. There was a problem, so he had to move the hit.

"Beaner, let the assassin takeout the watchman."

J. P. Beach says, "No problem, boss. The watchman doesn't have a clue. He's basically useless. My people blinded the fire system and the video system isn't working either. The warning systems won't work. They'll shutoff the fire sprinklers before the final match hits the fuse. These guys know their business."

On East Street the lookout reported a lucky break. Brenda Clark arrived at Richard Stern's house in Fairport Harbor.

The plan was shifting back and forth. The godfather ordered Boris and Lou to follow the toughs into position.

The godfather tells the assassin he's to takeout the watchman. Franco will show up there like he usually does.

The godfather tells Beaner to watch the assassin do the dirty work. Beaner's men can start the fire at midnight.

Franco and Miss Porter arrived at Stern's house. It was eight o'clock in the evening. Boris calls the godfather with the news.

The godfather says, "Wait for Franco and his woman to leave. You standby and watch the house. Don't do anything."

Boris says, "The boys are ready. We can get the whole bunch."

Angrily, the godfather shouts, "Wait, I say! Do nothing!"

Boris answers, "OK, boss."

"Go in when I give the order. Richard Stern, work him over, just as we planned. Make him drink beer and whiskey, so it's in his blood. Have the boys take Clark and Stern to Lake Erie. Just make sure Stern has alcohol in his system before they drown. Boris, you and Lou just watch from the road. Don't get involved."

Boris agrees.

A cold sweat overtakes Cambello because of the excitement. He was a little upset because the hit on Franco didn't take place as planned. The backup plan to hit Franco would be used. The clockwork instructions were off to a bad start. It was like an omen.

It was 8: 45PM when Boris calls, "Franco and the woman are leaving."

Cambello says, "Watch them leave. I don't want any bad luck right now. Things are happening all at once."

Boris says again, "Now they're leaving in his car."

The godfather says, "Don't panic, you just wait. We have time. Do nothing unless you hear from me."

After two hours, the godfather looked at his watch. It was a half hour before midnight.

"OK, Boris, do it just like we planned."

Boris barks in a low voice, "The girlfriend is leaving!"

The godfather asks, "What's happening?"

As Brenda was walking from Stern's house, a man grabbed her from behind as she was about to open her car door. A low power shock from a stun gun paralyzed her for a moment. She was quickly gagged. Duct tape bound her hands and feet as she was pushed into the backseat of her car. She couldn't move as he ripped off her shirt.

Brenda started to get feeling back. She could see his white goat skinned gloves rubbing on her. The rough texture of the gloves left marks on her shoulders as he tried to pull on her bra straps. His desire to have some fun by feeling her breasts pulled his attention away from his partners. She rolled away from him. Realizing his mistake, he stopped before he got carried away.

Boris says to the godfather, "Shorty got her, boss, no problem."

Stern thought he heard a car door slam. He looked out the window. A white caddy was parked next to Brenda's car. He thought he saw a man get out of Brenda's car. He waited for a few second or more; the man was getting inside her car as if to drive.

As the man moved to the car door, another man was almost inside his front door. Shocked that Brenda didn't lock the front door, Stern tried dialing for police on his cell phone. He held down on the white speed dial number on his phone as the thug got in and overpowered him sending the phone crashing on the hardwood floor. The cell phone battery fell out at the same time.

Monica Micovich's phone rang twice as she spied the phone number. It was Richard Stern's phone number that popped up. That was a major surprise to her.

Thoughts race around in Monica's head; she called back. There was no answer. She looked up his home phone number and dialed it. Richard's house phone was dead.

Monica hit speed dial again. It was to her partner, Paula Gavalia.

Paula answers, "Hello, Monica, it's a little late isn't it. What's wrong?"

Monica says, "Richard called, maybe by accident. I have a bad feeling. His home phone is dead. He might be drunk, but I'm headed over to his house. I'm not taking any chances. I really think something is wrong, not sure what's going on, partner. Do you want to have a look?"

Paula says, "Sure."

Monica says, "Michael is sleeping, but I'll check on him first. I'll meet you at Richard's house. Will you park on Fifth Street? I don't want him thinking I'm checking up on him."

"Knowing Mr. Stern," Paula responds, "I'll get my weapon, Monica."

Trying to calm the air, Monica says, "We might be jumping the gun. Don't think it's bad, but bring it and your cuffs."

After cutting the phone line, two more men piled into Stern's house in rapid succession, one thug waited in Brenda's car after taking care of her. They moved like clockwork. As Stern tried to dial 911 a man slapped his home phone away.

He knocked Stern down with a fist to his body. They bounced him around the family room, telling him to keep quiet or they would finish off his girlfriend. Then they forced Stern to have a drink of whiskey. The beer and whiskey was flowing between the boys as they were having some fun with Mr. Stern. He was at their mercy, overmatched in size and weight.

"We hear you like to stir up the Tea Party people." The hoodlum says.

Stern knew he was in deep trouble. Only ten minutes had passed.

Arriving one after the other, they communicated by cell phone. Because it was almost midnight the street light provided enough light for the agents to see two cars in his drive. A man was in one car. Something was going on at Stern's place.

Paula parked on Fifth Street and jumped out of her car when she heard a thud coming from Stern's first floor room. She crept close to the back of the house and listened to the people inside.

Monica pulled into the neighbor's drive and drove up the driveway to the garage, acting as if she lived there. She waited for Paula to move in. Paula crawled on her belly to Brenda's car. At that point she surprised the mugger holding Brenda. Paula put her pistol to the man's head. Her words were straightforward.

"You feel it. Keep your mouth closed. Put your hand on the steering wheel."

He complied as he felt the steel barrel of the Glock 26 on his neck. She cuffed each wrist to the steering wheel. Paula began to untied Brenda and whispered to her to keep quiet.

"We're FBI agents, are you ok?" Brenda nodded, ok.

Paula says, "I'm going to free you."

Brenda understood. She was frightened and still in shock.

Down the street Boris started the car as he watched the plan start to fall apart.

Lou says, "Let's go, Boris. We're out of here."

Boris started the caddy and turned around. He turned on Third Street heading west to High Street. From there they made their way out of town.

Paula waved to her partner to move in. Monica moved like a cat in the night. She heard the men laughing inside. She could see Stern was lying on his back. Having fun, the hoodlums poured whiskey into his mouth.

"Drink up old man, you and your girlfriend are going for a ride." says the thug.

Stern tried to turn his head as the mobster punched him on the face. He commanded him again as the others laughed.

"Have a drink with us old man."

Monica turned the door knob. It wasn't locked. She could hear the action inside as she entered the foyer. She crept slowly. Her next movement was timely as blood poured from Stern's nose.

The mobster said, "Have a beer, Mr. Stern" as he poured beer in his face.

The hoodlum says, "Man, you don't look well."

The first thug Monica greeted was no match for the taekwondo artist. Grabbing the tall black man by the wrist Monica stood him straight up with a one-two chop to the Adam's apple, the nose, and finally the wrist as he tried to pull his gun. The gun flew from his hand. It landed in the foyer.

Her speed was superior to the heavier second man. A foot between his legs forced him to grab his groin. He was in pain. Tears poured from his eyes as he doubled over. Looking up, he saw Monica's other foot greet him. Full force, the kick almost sent him to a back flip. He was stunned.

In the center of the room Richard grabbed the third man. Although Richard was pinned down on his back and the thug was using his face as a punching bag the assailant couldn't get away. The hoodlum buried his fist into Richard's cheek, while trying to fee himself from Richard's clutch.

Blood was now flowing from Richard's mouth. He lost his grip and was nearly unconscious when Monica sent the third mobster holding Stern flying into the wall. Her kick landed on his jaw twisting his neck in a sharp almost inconceivable direction.

She whirled around with lightning speed and planted a foot to the temple of the first man. The second man recovered. He started kicking Richard as he tried to recover. Monica cut him down with a flurry of hand chops and a swinging foot blow. The final rip hit him in the windpipe. This completely eliminated Richard's dire situation.

Richard and Monica's adrenalin was flowing, though he only could watch as he tried to rise from the floor. Stern was no marshal arts master, nothing like the swift moving agent.

She tore through the three mobsters like they were freshmen wrestlers meeting a pro. The speed at which she covered the room with hand and feet maneuvers left the thugs broken. Paula hailed the local police by cell phone.

After checking for weapons, Monica handcuffed the three men's wrists together with tie wraps.

Monica went to Richard's side, checking his pulse, she dialed 911 and requested police and an ambulance. They were already on their way. In less than two minutes the house was covered by Fairport Harbor police and deputy sheriffs. An ambulance arrived next. Paula identified herself and her partner. She explained the situation to the first responders.

It all happened so fast. Richard heard the ambulance pull up and the medical team was in the family room.

Stern said that two of the toughs pushed him as they explained their beef. They didn't want Stern or his girlfriend joining with the Tea Party folks or helping Franco with the Sports Park.

The four hoodlums stuck to their story. They were there to rob the place.

Chapter 34

ASSASSIN AND FIRE

Bingo was over by 10 o'clock that night. The hotel wasn't going to have any guests until the weekend, so it was closed.

At eleven twenty Franco dropped Simone off at the apartment after going out to see a movie. As he usually does, he drove to the Sports Park to make sure everything was secure for the night.

The assassin screwed a silencer onto the barrel of his Beretta .40 caliber handgun. Cold and calculating, as he double checked his weapon, he crept out of the bushes and made his way to the guardhouse. As the watchman stood puffing on a cigarette behind the guardhouse, the assassin subdued the man with one shot. The watchman fell onto his back, morally wounded out of sight. The fatal shot ended his life with the cigarette still burning, hanging from his lips.

The assassin spotted a car turning into the Sports Park. It was Franco's car. When Franco drove past the watchman's station, he thought it was strange that the night watchman wasn't in the guardhouse, but he was probably walking around the complex.

The assassin waited to see which building entrance Franco would use. As Franco went inside the gambling hall he left the door open to air out the place.

Only two night lights were illuminating the hall. Franco visually inspected the gambling hall. He walked over to the guest ledger near the front door to see how many people signed in.

The assassin moved quickly. His dirty work didn't take but a few seconds. He fired a single shot at thirty feet.

Franco went down, shot in the back.

The assassin signaled for the arsonists to begin their work. He fled the scene, driving away as if nothing happened.

The Iranians stepped over the body of Franco, but took the time to add insult to the dead owner's corpse. They sprinkled the body with gun powder as if it was incense.

Their work was starting in earnest. The first fire was about to be started in the casino hall. It would spread fast to the hotel hallway and into the hotel because of the accelerant. Then explosives would rock the Sports complex.

The godfather's Middle Eastern fire starters went overboard in their assignment, not understanding the words of the boss's lieutenant. Beaner told them to make sure the 'hall' burns down, but he was referring to the casino hall not 'all burns down.' The fire would go well beyond the intended targets.

Beaner didn't follow the Iranians. He didn't realize the arsonist were planting charges throughout the complex. The arsonists moved through the buildings with bottles of butane, gun powder, and oxygen cylinders. A stream of gunpowder and a cell phone fuse was employed as a backup in two areas of the hotel.

Finally, a candle was lit in one room and a butane cylinder was set on a table and cracked open in the room well away from the candle. The butane would eventually slink to the ground and ignite.

After all was set, they lit the gunpowder fuse and drove away. Beaner watched them leave and he followed as the first charge exploded.

A monster fire broke out in the smaller gambling hall which quickly spread to the hotel and large casino. The blaze roared as accelerant drove the flames across the hall to the other buildings. In a matter of five minutes the hotel and gambling hall were covered in flames. The inferno was so intense the aluminum bleachers were melting. It lit up the sky for boaters to see on Lake Erie.

The flames licked the sky. People driving on Fairport Nursery Road looked on as the fire sent a plume of smoke high in the nighttime air. Fire on the three top floors of the hotel was burning out of control. The fire could be seen moving curtains as if signaling rescue personnel. The hotel was engulfed in minutes with no sprinkler system working.

The sirens were blaring as the fire trucks roared out of Fairport Harbor. As Stern was being transported to the Concord hospital, he could hear the radio dispatch communicating information about the Sports Park fire. Painesville Township's fire department was rolling as well as Painesville City's fire trucks.

Back in Chicago the godfather was kicking back, waiting for the good news.

Boris didn't want to call the godfather until he was out of Ohio. He knew the boss would be furious when he was told the job fell apart.

The news from the assassin was relayed to the godfather and shortly after more news arrived about the fire. The godfather turned toward his girlfriend and declared.

"They're not going to be gambling at the Sports Park after tonight. I hear there is trouble. The place is on fire. Just for good measure say good bye to Franco and charity gambling.

She says, "Goodbye, Mr. Franco!"

With a smile on his face the godfather says, "We play rough or should I say, don't play with guns or fire. We have to do things the Chicago way."

Chapter 35
THE AMERICAN SPIRIT LIVES

Franco was gone. After the burial, Simone went back to Oregon. Brenda Clark and Simone patched up their differences, because of the tragedy. The mourning went on for weeks. The fire finished charity gambling and the Sports Park.

Questions surrounded the whole event. Murder and suspicion were murmured. Some people said that Franco burned down his place because of money problems. This callous rumor made people angry, especially those who helped Franco.

The body of the watchman signaled foul play. Fire inspectors determined arson was definitely involved. Forensic evidence proved the fire was deliberately set. The reason for the fire wasn't fully understood. People were bidding to buy the Sports Park which was a total loss. This kept them from being suspects.

Nearly everyone looked at the symbolic meaning of the fire. It was like a piece of America was gone, just like the Erie Indians and the old Diamond Shamrock Company.

Franco had a dream. The spirit of the property would rise again. Some other big enterprise would build on the property.

Brenda and Richard were saved from the people who had no morals. The Chicago godfather would find out he wasn't immortal.

Agent Monica Micovich and Paula Gavalia were assigned the case. They were FBI agents the godfather feared the most.

The godfather already had tough luck trying to eliminate Agent

Monica Micovich. At one point her partner, Agent Gavalia, was closing in on Mr. Mahdi. She hid a secret that was to crack the case wide open. Now that they were investigating the fire, events really escalated. Cambello was feeling the heat.

An arms journal of transactions was missing from the bank and this caused Cambello and Mahdi to wonder if Agent Gavalia took it. Sargon Mahdi convinced himself that he misplaced it or it was accidentally put in the shredder. However, doubt still stirred in his mind. Sargon wasn't sure.

Mr. Mahdi had a big worry on his hands.

The Sports Park fire opened a can of worms for Cambello. Even though Franco's death was a consolation prize, nothing seemed to be going his way. His party was under assault all over America.

His experiences with the Cleveland FBI, especially with the two female agents, had always caused him trouble.

Agents Monica Micovich and Paula Gavalia were snooping around. They were asking questions about people making offers to buy Franco's property.

Much information was pointing to the very bank in Chicago and Detroit that had an interest in Franco's property.

Political action groups were receiving stimulus money. A big scandal was caught on video and distributed to TV stations. Some media outlets tried to down play the situation, but the Fox crew was working, digging up the truth, the real story.

Two Weeks Later

About two weeks went by and Cambello received a call from one of his men.

"We have some news for you, boss. One of the FBI agents you had a problem with was involved in an auto accident. Her car went off the road and she didn't survive."

The godfather asks, "Who was it?"

"Agent Paula Gavalia, except that wasn't her real name."

Not paying attention, the godfather asks, "Who?"

The lieutenant says, "The newspaper said Agent Paula Gavelda. She was a person with an interesting life.

"Better listen to this boss. She had a big family of brothers and sister. It said she was dedicated to helping people overcome addictions. What really got me looking at this article was her background in espionage. Here's the big news in the article. It also said, also known as, Agent Paula Gavalia."

The lieutenant repeats, "Agent Paula Gavalia was Paula Gavelda. She was killed in an auto accident."

The godfather says, "Something isn't right. I remember that name. Mahdi couldn't find the arms journal. It was about the time when a foxy blond, a tax auditor, was looking at his bank records. He said her name was Paula Gavelda. He was telling me on the phone; he wanted a date with her. She was a beauty."

"Boss, it says her name is Paula Gavelda."

The godfather asks, "Are you sure about the name?"

The lieutenant says, "Boss, her name was in the obituary column of the local newspaper. It says her best friend and partner was Agent Monica Micovich. She gave the eulogy according to the article. They worked together at the Cleveland FBI office.

"It looks like they won awards as Homeland Security Superstars. It says, 'Agent Paula Gavelda's lifestyle will always be remembered.'"

The godfather says, "Mr. Mahdi said he lost one of our records. Our arms deals were covered in that book. Mahdi blew it off by saying it probably got shredded.

"Paula Gavelda, are you sure?"

"Yes, boss."

The godfather says, "We got trouble. She took the journal."

The next day the godfather's revelation was realized. The Federal Bureau of Investigation, the Bureau of Alcohol, Tobacco, and Firearms, the National Security Agency, and the National Intelligence Service were at his South Chicago villa in force.

Supervisor Cliff Moses and Agent Micovich served him with an arrest warrant. He was charged with illegal arms sales, racketeering, and a host of other charges.

Monica was staring him down as she disclosed the truth and read him his rights.

"You're organization and the greedy politicians can't steal freedom from the people, Mr. Cambello. We'll eventually find all the crooks. America will survive."

The most incriminating evidence was received by U. S. Mail. It was a package addressed to Agent Monica Micovich.

John Gavelda mailed it to Agent Micovich. Mr. Gavelda said one of his sisters had never mailed the package, so he did. On the return address of the package was written P. Gavelda. Inside the package was a ledger, a journal of arms sales with dates listed. The ledger came from a Detroit bank. Krugerrands were shipped to Mr. Cambello's Chicago bank to pay for the weapon shipments. The Chicago style of doing business was coming to a halt.

Julius Cambello should have realized his fear. The agents had his number and the other fact. The Tea Party folks would make sure the Second Civil War didn't happen.

The End

LaVergne, TN USA
19 December 2010
209366LV00007B/11/P